The second decade : voyages

Author: Hoobler, Dorothy.
Reading Level: 4.2 MG
Point Value: 4.0
ACCELERATED READER QUIZ# 2993

P9-DVR-468

THE
SECOND
DECADE

Voyages

2000

1990

1980

1970

1960

1950

1940

1930

1920

1910

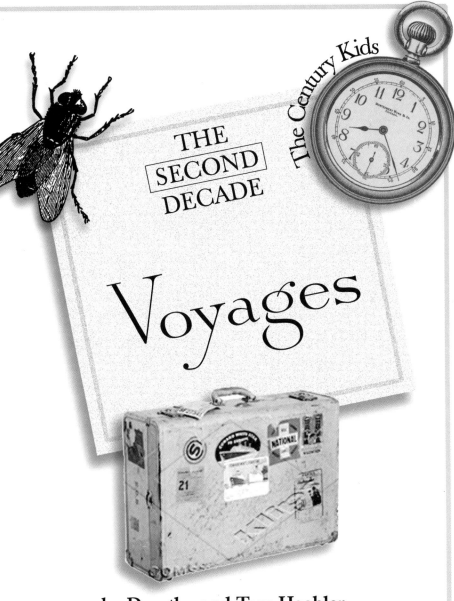

THE SECOND DECADE

The Century Kids

Voyages

by Dorothy and Tom Hoobler

The Millbrook Press • Brookfield, Connecticut

For Teresa Bucchieri

Hoobler, Dorothy.
The second decade: voyages/by Dorothy and Thomas Hoobler.
p. cm.–(The century kids)
Summary: An Italian immigrant boy joins the large
Aldrich family as they stage a women's suffrage play
and listen to messages on the wireless radio about
the ocean voyage of the Titanic.
ISBN 0–7613–1601–9 (lib. bdg.)
[1. Family life Fiction. 2. Theater Fiction. 3. Italian American
Fiction. 4. Women–Suffrage Fiction.] I. Hoobler, Thomas.
II. Title. III. Series: Hoobler, Dorothy. Century kids.
PZ7.H76227Sf   2000
[Fic]–dc21   99-37397   CIP

Published by The Millbrook Press, Inc.
2 Old New Milford Road
Brookfield, Connecticut 06804
www.millbrookpress.com

THE
SECOND
DECADE

Voyages

Strike!

MARCH 13, 1912

NELL COULD HEAR THE STRIKERS LONG BEFORE she could see them. The sounds of several hundred people singing and chanting carried a long way. Somebody was banging on a drum, too. Nell craned her head to see down the street. But the marching crowd still wasn't in sight.

"It sounds like they're coming up Grove Street," said Nell's older sister, Peggy. "When they turn the corner, they'll come right toward us."

Peggy had set up her camera next to the small bridge that led to the textile mill where the strikers worked. "If they march on the mill, they'll have to cross here," Peggy told Nell. "I could get a photograph that any magazine would love to have."

Nell

Peggy had already sold some of her photographs to magazines and newspapers. Most of them had been pictures of actors and actresses. They had been easy to get, because their family, the Aldriches, had been in the theater for at least four generations.

But when Peggy heard about the textile workers' strike in Lawrence, Massachusetts, she decided it was her big chance. "The whole country is talking about this strike," she had said at dinner two nights ago. "People will want to see what it looks like."

"That's true," their father had said, "but it could be dangerous. I understand that the police found boxes of dynamite stored in a cellar."

"It was proved that the dynamite didn't belong to any of the union members," Peggy replied.

Nell had seen Papa and Mama exchange glances. She knew what that meant. Peggy was nearly twenty-three, and it was hard for them to keep her from doing whatever she wanted to do. She had graduated from Wellesley College, and now earned her own money taking photographs. She still took roles in plays, too.

Nell could see that her older sister was determined to go. Peggy's lips were pressed together and her eyes flashed. Nell had practiced doing that herself in front of a mirror. She liked to imitate people. It was good training for being on the stage.

Then Papa had said something surprising. "Why don't you take Nell along, then?"

Peggy's eyes lost their flash. "Nell?" She looked at her younger sister. "She's only twelve. She shouldn't be going to something like this."

"I thought you said it wasn't dangerous," Papa said mildly.

Nell understood. Papa was clever. He didn't want to get into an argument with Peggy. But he knew she wouldn't let anything happen to Nell. So she would stay away from anything that might be dangerous.

It was tiresome, really, Nell thought. When your only sister is eleven years older than you are, she acts like she can boss you around. But this time, Nell would use it to her advantage. "Oh, take me along, won't you, Peggy?" she had said. "I can help you take the photographs."

Peggy glared at her. The only way she could refuse to take Nell was to admit it was dangerous. And of course that would give Papa a good reason to keep Peggy from going.

So here they were, right in the middle of what the Boston newspaper called "a powder keg

Peggy

waiting to explode." Nell could hardly wait to see the strikers.

She felt perfectly safe, for she and Peggy had gone inside the factory earlier that morning. Hundreds of soldiers with rifles and bayonets were there, ready to keep the strikers from destroying the machinery.

That was how the strike began, six weeks earlier. When the workers found out that their pay was to be reduced, some of them jumped up and started to break the looms on which they worked. By the end of the day, all of them had left their jobs and gone out on strike.

Nell had heard people say that the strikers should all be put in jail. Mr. Pomeroy, the mayor of Lake Chohobee, Maine, the town where she lived, announced that he wouldn't tolerate any strikes. Of course, there weren't any factories in their town. It wasn't anything like Lawrence, Massachusetts.

Lawrence was a gloomy place. The huge brick mill buildings squatted next to the river looking more like prisons than places where people would go to work all day. The rest of the town was worse—all unpainted wooden buildings that looked as if a strong wind would blow them over. Nell had read that none of the mill owners or managers lived in Lawrence. Only the workers did. She understood why. Nobody would live here who didn't have to.

Suddenly the noise Nell had been listening to grew clearer. She turned her head to see a throng of people coming her way. Many of them were waving American flags and banners with slogans like FAIR PAY FOR A DAY'S WORK, FOUR LOAVES OF BREAD, and BREAD AND ROSES. Some of the banners were in languages that Nell couldn't read.

As the crowd approached, Nell said to Peggy, "They don't look very dangerous at all."

Peggy didn't reply. She was already aiming her Speed Kodak and snapping pictures. Nell noticed that even though it was a cold day, almost none of the strikers wore overcoats. There were many women and children in the crowd, but they too just wore flimsy dresses, ragged sweaters, or thin jackets buttoned all the way to the collar. Wasn't it strange that even though they made cloth, they couldn't afford coats? Their hands were bare as well. Self-consciously, Nell made fists inside the warm woolen mittens that she wore. She shivered, even though her woolen coat was thick and had a fur collar.

Out of the corner of her eye, Nell saw something else move. She looked and saw a squadron of blue-jacketed police come around the side of the factory. They were a lot more scary than the strikers were. They carried billy clubs and looked tough and angry.

As soon as the police came into sight, the strikers began to hoot and shout at them. Instead of falling back, they seemed to surge forward like a wave rushing onto a beach.

Nell suddenly realized that she and Peggy were standing right at the spot where the two crowds were going to meet. She nudged her sister. "Peggy, I think we'd better move."

Peggy paid no attention. She was concentrating on getting pictures of the crowd of strikers, which suddenly looked more threatening to Nell. Those in front were waving the flags and banners as if they wanted to wrap them around the police.

Nell caught sight of one boy who looked no older than she was. Black curly hair stuck out on both sides of the gray cap he wore. His trousers and shirt were mismatched—one brown, the other dark blue with white stripes. But even from where Nell stood, she could see the flash in his eyes. The same kind of flash that Peggy had when she got angry. The boy was holding up a banner and marching forward with determination. It was clear that he intended to cross the bridge with it. Very likely the rest of the strikers would follow.

Glancing in the other direction, Nell saw that the police were just as determined to stop them. She poked Peggy harder and pointed toward the police. Peggy looked and turned her camera

toward them. "Thanks, Nell," she said. "This will be a great shot."

"I didn't mean that," Nell told her. She had to raise her voice because the crowd was getting louder as it came closer. "We're going to be—" But the sound of clanging metal cut her off. The first strikers had reached the bridge and were running across it. She looked for the bright-eyed boy, but didn't see him. Some older men had passed him and were now in the lead.

Then the police reached the place where Peggy and Nell were standing. They weren't considerate at all. Peggy gave a cry as one of the policemen shoved her aside so that he could get to the bridge. Nell grabbed hold of a metal railing that protected people from falling into the river. Otherwise she would have been swept along in the crush.

As she watched, the police ran onto the bridge and began swinging their clubs. The banners, held high above the marchers, folded and then collapsed. The strikers fought back with their fists. Because the bridge was so narrow, only a few people were actually fighting, while others were crushed up behind them.

"Nell!" It was Peggy's voice. Nell turned and saw her struggling toward the railing. She managed to get up next to Nell. "Hold onto me," Peggy said. "I want to lean over to take a clear shot."

Nell stared at her. "Don't you think we ought to move farther away?"

"Why?" Peggy asked. "No one is going to attack us."

Nell shrugged and put her arms around her sister's waist. Peggy bent over the railing and aimed her camera at the fighting on the bridge.

Just then, Nell saw the bright-eyed boy again. His banner was torn and dirty now. Even so, he was still struggling to carry it across the bridge. Fascinated, Nell watched him avoid the blows of the police by ducking under them. He slipped past the fighting by sticking close to the side. At last he reached the far end of the bridge.

That was where a policeman noticed him. The burly officer raised his club. The boy's back was turned and he couldn't see the danger.

"Watch out!" Nell shouted.

The boy heard her. He whirled and ducked, but the policeman's club hit his shoulder. The boy nearly fell, but as the policeman reached for him, he slipped out of the man's grasp and ran. The policeman started after him. They were heading right toward Nell and Peggy.

Peggy was still leaning over the railing and didn't notice what was happening. Nell pulled her back. Peggy turned to complain just as the boy ran past. Then Nell stepped into the policeman's path, pulling Peggy with her.

With a grunt, the policeman ran into them, and all three crashed to the ground. Peggy screamed–first in surprise and then anger as she realized what had happened. "How dare you!" she cried to the policeman.

With no apology, he jumped to his feet and resumed the chase. Nell could see, however, that the boy had a good head start. She doubted he would be caught.

Peggy regained her feet and said, "What a brute." She examined her camera.

"Is it all right?" Nell asked.

"It seems to be working," Peggy replied. "I'm nearly out of film anyway." She looked suspiciously at Nell. "If I didn't know better, I'd say you put us into the policeman's way on purpose."

"I did," Nell confessed. "You didn't see this boy he was chasing. He was so young. I had to do something."

"We're not supposed to get involved in the strike," Peggy told her. She pointed her camera in the direction of the bridge and took another picture. By now, the strikers had fallen back to their end, and were chanting and singing once more. "That's the last of the film," said Peggy. "I think we'd better get back to Boston so we can catch the afternoon train to Kennebunk."

"There haven't been any bombs going off yet," Nell said in disappointment.

"Wasn't being run over by a policeman enough excitement for you?"

"It wasn't funny," Nell said. "You didn't see him hit this boy."

Peggy packed her camera in its case and they walked toward the train station. "Do you hope the strikers will win?" Nell asked.

Peggy nodded. "Yes, I think their cause is a just one," she said. "But they shouldn't use violence or destroy property."

"What if the other side uses violence against *them*?"

Peggy thought for a moment. "Perhaps if women could vote, we would have leaders who wouldn't ignore the conditions in the mills. They would prevent either side from needing to use violence."

Nell nodded. She knew Peggy supported the votes-for-women movement. Last year, Peggy had carried petitions in favor of women's suffrage in Maine. But the proposal was voted down. Because, of course, only men were allowed to cast votes.

Something interrupted her thoughts. It was a noise. Nell caught hold of Peggy's arm. "Did you hear something?"

"It's the strikers," Peggy said. "They're still chanting."

"No." Nell looked around. "It wasn't . . ." She took a few steps back and looked down an alleyway between two rundown buildings. In the shadows, she saw a small figure slumped against a wall. She recognized the striped blue shirt and brown pants. It was the boy who had run from the policeman.

TWO

Getting Rocco Out

"ARE YOU ALL RIGHT?" NELL CALLED.

The boy turned his head to look at her. The bright eyes were filled with tears, and his face was contorted in pain. "It is not too bad," he said.

Nell called her sister. "That's the boy the policeman hit," she said. "He's hurt."

Peggy stood at the entrance to the alley, uncertain what to do. "Can we help you get home?" she asked.

The boy shook his head.

"We can take him to a hospital," Nell said.

Peggy nodded. "Yes, that would be best." She stepped into the alley, and Nell followed. Carefully, they helped the boy to his feet. Nell could see a grimace of pain run across his face.

"No hospital," he said. He had an accent. Most of the workers in the cloth mills were immigrants.

"You're hurt," Peggy explained. "Your arm may be broken, and a doctor must set it."

Firmly, the boy shook his head. "The police go to the hospital after workers have a march," he explained. "They put people who hurt in jail."

"Put them in jail?" Peggy replied. "Oh, no. That can't be true."

He nodded. "Yes, true. Happen to friend of mine."

He pushed their hands away so that he could stand by himself. "I go now," he said. "Thank you." But as he started to walk away, the pain in his shoulder nearly caused him to fall. Once more, Nell and Peggy had to hold him up.

"I know," Peggy said. "We'll take him back to Boston on the train."

She spoke loudly to him, as if he were hard of hearing. "We'll go to Boston! You understand? You can go to a hospital there."

Weakly, he nodded.

Walking slowly and stopping to let him rest, they made their way to the train station. A guard looked suspiciously at them as they entered, but said nothing. They got the boy settled on a bench, and Peggy went off to buy tickets.

He leaned back and closed his eyes. Curious, Nell looked him over. The only immigrants she knew were from Ireland, and this boy looked nothing like them. His skin was olive-colored and he had soft features. His clothes were even more worn-out than she'd thought. His trousers had been patched at both knees. Somebody had sewed up a tear in his shirt, but had done it badly.

"What's your name?" she asked.

His eyes opened again. She could see that he didn't quite trust her. "Rocco," he said. "What yours?"

"Nell," she told him.

"Nil?" he repeated.

"No, Nell," she said. "My mother said if I'd been a boy, it would have been Noel. I was born just at the turn of the twentieth century."

Rocco

He smiled at her. His teeth were very white against his skin. "Turn of century? You mean at the time of first day in the year?"

"Yes, just at midnight."

He pointed to his chest. "Me too."

She stared. "No, I mean . . . how do you know?"

He waved his hand. "Same way you know. My mama say it to me. She heard the church bell when I was born."

"Your mother?" Nell frowned. "Where is your mother?"

His smile disappeared, and he turned away from her. "She die," he muttered softly.

Embarrassed, Nell didn't know what to say. She wanted to ask more questions, but was afraid of hurting him further. She looked up and saw with relief that Peggy was approaching.

"Did you get Rocco a ticket?" Nell asked.

"Yes," Peggy said in a low voice. "But I had to say he was my brother. They're stopping children from getting on the train if they look like strikers."

Nell glanced at Rocco, and then at Peggy. "I know," Peggy said. "He doesn't look much like our brother, does he?"

"If we could get him some other clothes, it might help."

"We haven't time," Peggy said. "The train leaves in ten minutes. What did you say his name is?"

"Rocco."

"I have an idea." Peggy leaned over. "Rocco, we have to disguise you." She took the cap off his head. He looked worried as she put it into her handbag.

"Disguise?" he repeated.

"Give him your hat, Nell," Peggy said. "And take off your coat."

Nell blinked. "My coat? But it's cold."

"We're inside. You can get it back once we're on the train."

Nell thought back to the moment when she felt sorry for the strikers because they had no coats. Well, now she had a chance to see what it was like.

Her fur hat was a perfect fit for Rocco. They had to drape the coat over his shoulders because his arm hurt too much to get into the sleeve. But when they buttoned it up, you couldn't see his shabby clothes. Rocco looked down at himself and rolled his eyes. Nell couldn't help laughing.

Then she pointed to his shoes. They were coming apart, and the leather looked as if it hadn't ever been shined. "I know," said Peggy. "But we can't do anything about them. We'll just have to hope no one notices."

In a few minutes, the train arrived, and they went out onto the platform. Fortunately, they had no luggage except Peggy's camera case. The conductor was standing on the platform by the first passenger car. He waved them forward to board it, but they got on the car behind it. They found two double seats facing each other and sat down. Peggy put her camera case on the floor to hide Rocco's feet.

With relief, they heard the conductor cry, "All aboard!" and then felt a jolt as the train started forward.

"We're safe now," Nell said softly.

"Just act naturally when the conductor comes for our tickets," replied Peggy.

Nell looked across the seat at Rocco, who was sitting next to Peggy. The hat was pulled down almost to his eyes, and the coat collar covered everything up to his nose. He looked like a baby wrapped up tight in a blanket. She couldn't help but smile. When he saw that, he wiggled his eyebrows at her and she nearly laughed out loud.

When the conductor came, Peggy handed him the tickets. Nell tried to think of how to act naturally. It was difficult when you weren't supposed to attract attention. Nothing like being on stage. But the conductor punched the tickets and handed them back without a word.

They breathed a sigh of relief as he passed on down the aisle. "Too hot," Rocco whispered to Peggy. She unbuttoned the coat and took the fur hat off his head.

"I thank you," he said, running his hand through his hair. "I leave you when the train stops."

"No, you must get treatment for your shoulder," said Peggy.

"It is not so hurting now," he said. But Nell noticed that he still winced when he moved that side of his body.

"We should notify your parents," Peggy told him.

He turned his head away. "His mother is dead," Nell told Peggy. "I don't think he lives with his father, either."

Rocco nodded.

"Where do you live, then?" Peggy asked.

"In rooming house," he said. "Dollar a week to stay in big room. Other boys in same place. Eight of us. Another two dollars, I get meals too."

Peggy shook her head. "But you're no older than Nell is."

"He says he's exactly the same age," Nell said. She wanted to ask him more about his birthday. She'd never met anybody else who was born at the very start of the century.

Peggy wasn't interested in that. "I mean, why were you working in the cloth mill?"

Rocco looked puzzled. "Have to work," he explained. "Need money."

"Children your age shouldn't be working," Peggy said firmly.

"Some younger than me," he said. "Girls too."

"We saw them in the demonstration," said Nell.

"I don't think the union should let children march at all," Peggy said. "It's too dangerous. You were hurt, and others could have been too."

Rocco looked at her. "There was a girl in the factory where I was," he said. "She supposed to clear the thread from the machine when it stops.

They use girls for that because their hands are fast. One day, this girl got her hand caught. Fingers and hand all torn and bloody. Later we heard doctor had to cut off her hand. Factory owner gave her parents fifty dollars."

He looked at Peggy. "What you think of that, eh? Fifty dollars . . . for a hand."

"It's disgusting," said Peggy.

"And then last month they make our pay lower," he said. "So we strike. Even if we boys, girls, men, women—we all work, all strike."

Nell had been listening, fascinated by all this. "I would have struck too," she said.

"You can't go back there," Peggy said. "Isn't there someone who will take care of you?"

"No worry," he said. "In Boston I find a job."

"That isn't what I mean," Peggy replied. She took a deep breath. "First, we will see a doctor. And then . . . " She hesitated. "You can come home with us. For now."

"Really?" Nell said. "Do you think—" She glanced at Rocco.

Peggy understood what she meant. "Mother and Father won't mind. I'll explain it to them."

Rocco shook his head. "Is not necessary," he said. "Many jobs in Boston. I will be . . . okay." He smiled as he remembered the right word.

But Peggy insisted. And as Nell knew from experience, Peggy usually got her way. As soon as the train arrived in Boston, they took Rocco to a doctor's office. Because the doctor was the father of one of Peggy's college classmates, they didn't need an appointment.

Fortunately, Rocco only had bruises. Nothing was broken. The doctor gave him some pills to lessen the pain.

Once they left the doctor's, Peggy steered them toward a fancy men's clothing store. A salesman immediately came up to them, and looked at Rocco as if he were going to set the place on fire. But his face changed when Peggy said, "I'm Peggy Aldrich. My Uncle Richard has an account here."

The salesman nodded his head with a smile. Uncle Richard was one of the most famous actors in America, and known for being a flashy dresser. "How can I help you today?" the man said.

"Dress him," Peggy said, pointing to Rocco. Nell put her hand over her mouth when she saw Rocco's expression. He looked more afraid than when he was running from the policeman.

The man grasped Rocco to keep him from running away. "Something . . . er, suitable for prep school?" the man asked Peggy.

Peggy frowned. "Maybe for an outing in the country," she said.

"I'll see what I can do."

Peggy and Nell sat on a sofa provided for customers, and another salesman brought them cups of tea. "Do you really think Mother and Father will let Rocco stay with us?" Nell asked.

"We have plenty of room," Peggy pointed out. "Grandpa built the house to hold everybody in the family, and guests besides. Rocco can be our guest. If he wants to work, there's plenty to do around the place. Horses, gardens, automobiles, and now Uncle Georgie's talking about buying an airplane."

"I don't think Rocco knows anything about airplanes," said Nell.

"Uncle Georgie would be glad to teach him," replied Peggy.

About half an hour later, the salesman brought Rocco back for display. The change was astonishing. He now wore a white shirt, tie, and sweater, along with tweed knickers and plaid socks. The salesman had fitted him with shiny new black leather shoes as well. Rocco kept trying to glimpse himself in one of the mirrors that lined the walls.

"He looks fine," Peggy said. "Do you have an overcoat and cap?"

The salesman brought those, too. Both were made of tan camel's hair.

"Shall I . . . dispose of the young man's other clothing?" asked the salesman.

"Yes," said Peggy.

"No," said Rocco. "I have something in the pocket."

The salesman left and returned with a small leather bag tied shut with a string. "Is this it?" he asked.

Rocco took it from him and put it into his overcoat. Nell wondered what could be inside, but she realized it would be impolite to ask.

As Peggy signed the charge account, Rocco took a good look in the mirror. He adjusted his cap, trying it first one way, then another. "What you think?" he asked Nell.

"Oh, you look very smart," she said.

He looked at himself again. "Look like this . . . I can't go back to the factory."

Yes, Nell thought. He was right. He wouldn't fit in there now. Rocco didn't sound as if he were completely happy about that.

THREE

Flies, Tennis Balls, and a Wireless

MARCH 13, 1912

PEGGY SENT A TELEGRAM TO LET THEIR FAMILY know when their train would be arriving. After they boarded, they went to the dining car and sat down at a table. Rocco picked up the menu and looked at both sides of it. He squinted like someone who needed glasses. With a sigh, he set the menu down and watched Peggy and Nell.

Nell realized he couldn't read it. "The club sandwich is very good," she told him.

He nodded with relief. "Yes, sandwich. I like sandwich."

While they waited to be served, Nell remembered what she'd been dying to tell Peggy. "Rocco

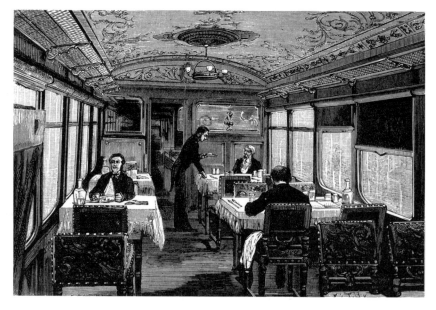

told me that he was born on the first day of the century. Just like me."

"Where were you born?" Peggy asked.

"In Italy," he said.

"How did you get to America?"

"Same way as everybody," he replied. "On a boat."

They laughed at that. "Did your parents come with you?"

He became silent again, looking down at the spotless white tablecloth. Nell was relieved when the waiter brought their sandwiches.

The club sandwich seemed to puzzle Rocco a little. He lifted the top slice of toast and examined it closely. Shrugging, he put it back and started to eat. In fact, he finished long before Peggy and Nell did. He took a sip of water and put the glass down.

"Did you enjoy your sandwich?" Nell asked.

"Yes," he said, but didn't sound enthusiastic.

"Was there something wrong with it?"

He spread his hands. "I see they did that to your sandwich too."

"What?"

"Burn the bread."

"Oh." Nell blinked. "That's toast."

"Toast." He repeated it. "I will remember. But then maybe the toast is supposed to make you not notice the tomato."

"Don't you like tomatoes?"

"Of course I like tomatoes," he said with a smile. "But this was not like a tomato we grow in Italy. It is like . . ." He waved his hands again. "You know the pictures they print in magazines?"

"Yes. That's what Peggy was doing today. Taking pictures for one."

He nodded. "And if you ate a picture of a tomato . . . would it taste the same?"

"As a real tomato? Why, no." Nell giggled at the thought of it.

"Then if you ever eat a real tomato, you will know that this was only a picture of one."

It wasn't long before the train arrived at Kennebunk. Michael, the family chauffeur, was waiting for them in the big green Winton to drive them back to Lake Chohobee. He looked Rocco over carefully. "Rocco will be staying with us for a while," said Peggy.

"I see," Michael said. "And is his luggage in the baggage car?"

"It will arrive later," Peggy replied.

Michael gave her a suspicious look. Years ago he had taught Peggy to ride horses. He sometimes told Nell, "I still have to keep your sister from falling off her high horse now and then." He was about the only person who tried to tell Peggy what to do—or not to do.

But this time, he just shrugged and made Rocco sit in the front seat with him. It didn't matter to Rocco. He kept looking from right to left as if he'd never been in an automobile before. Michael started to tell him about the controls and how fast the car could go. "Forty miles an hour," Rocco said, turning to tell Peggy and Nell.

"That's nothing," said Peggy. "If cousin Harry comes to visit, we'll send you driving with him. He goes twice as fast."

It was true. Harry drove in automobile races. Once, he'd driven a car faster than anybody else ever had, but Barney Oldfield broke his record two years ago. Harry was hoping to get it back at this year's big race at Indianapolis.

They reached the Aldrich estate, drove through the big iron gates, and came to a stop by the front door of the house. Rocco got out and looked around. "Ahhhhh," he said, taking a deep breath. Then he turned to Peggy and Nell. "You live here?"

They nodded.

"You are *nobiltá*, then."

"No, we're not nobility," Peggy said. She had learned some Italian in college. "Our grandfather was a famous actor, and he built this house."

They went inside while Michael put the car away. "See," Peggy said as they took off their coats in the front hall, "we don't even have a butler."

A girl with blond pigtails rushed into the hallway. She was carrying a small net in one hand and a glass jar in the other. "I heard the door open," she said. "You didn't let any flies in, did you?"

"This is our cousin Polly," Peggy said. "And no, Polly, we didn't. It's March, and all the flies are frozen."

"Not the ones indoors," she said. "I caught three more today." She held up the jar, and they could see three flies buzzing about.

Polly

Polly looked at Rocco. "Are you afraid of germs?"

He blinked and thought for a second. "No, they make war with France, not Italy."

"Not Germans," said Polly. "Germs. Tiny little creatures that make you sick. They ride around on the backs of flies."

"I never heard of them," said Rocco. He smiled and looked at Nell to see if she thought this was a joke too.

"Peggy saw some at college," Nell told him, trying to let him know Polly wasn't completely crazy. "But you need a microscope."

Polly drew closer to Rocco. "Promise me that if you see a fly, you'll tell me *right away*."

"I promise," he said solemnly.

Satisfied with that, Polly went off to the kitchen, ready to pounce on unsuspecting flies.

The others started up the big marble staircase. Nell explained, "Polly read an article in a magazine. Some doctor wrote it."

"Doctor Mallinson," Peggy said. "The article was called 'The Invisible World.' It frightened lots of people besides Polly. He thinks if we could wipe out flies, then germs would disappear from homes."

"In the factory," Rocco said, "if a fly bother us, we . . . " he couldn't think of the word, but slapped the railing on the staircase.

"Swat it," Peggy said. "Yes, that's what most people do. But Polly is a little persnickety. She thinks that swatting flies spreads the germs around more. So she catches them instead."

Nell giggled. "It's really because she hates the sight of squashed flies."

"What she do with the ones she catch?" Rocco asked.

"I think she's been storing them in the cellar," Nell said. "Bridget, the housekeeper, has been complaining awfully. She has all her canned fruit and vegetables down there."

As they walked down the second-floor hallway, Rocco stared at the theater posters that lined the walls. Peggy pointed to one. "That's grandfather," she said. "And over here is Uncle Richard as the Scarlet Pimpernel. He and Aunt Laura are in Europe right now." A little farther down the hall, she said, "This poster shows our parents—William and Anna Aldrich—when they were in *The Taming of the Shrew* together. You'll meet them later. And here's one of Aunt Maud as Ophelia. She retired from the stage to raise her children. Polly's one of them."

Rocco shook his head. "All of you are actors?" he asked.

"We don't have to be," said Peggy. "Uncle Georgie is an inventor. Of sorts. Our cousin Jack is in Germany, studying science. And as we told you, Harry races cars. Right now, I'm trying to decide whether I want to continue acting or devote my time to photography."

"Every summer the family puts on a play together," said Nell. "Grandpa built a theater on the grounds. If you're still here then . . . " She stopped and looked at Peggy.

"Oh, we'll find something for you to do," Peggy said. "Right now, I think we should give you a room. There's an empty one down here next to Freddy's."

As they neared the end of the hallway, they heard a thumping noise coming from inside the last room. It wasn't very loud, but it kept on going—ka-thump, ka-thump, ka-thump.

"Someone has a machine going in there," Rocco said.

Peggy frowned. "I don't think so." She opened the door. Inside was a girl who looked just like the girl they had met down-stairs. Only this one was batting a tennis ball against the wall. She leaped about the room, bouncing from the bed to the floor, as she returned the ball.

Rocco stared. "How'd she get up here?" he asked.

"Oh, this isn't Polly," Peggy explained. "It's her twin, Molly. Molly, come meet our guest Rocco."

Molly caught the tennis ball in her hand and turned. She gave Rocco a quick look. "Oh, my eye!" she exclaimed. "He's a striker, isn't he? You brought one of them home."

Peggy flushed. "Please don't tell anyone, Molly."

Molly

Molly nodded. "Oh, I see, Lee. You dressed him up. Keep it a secret from the old folks. Not bad, but can he talk English?"

"You are not like your sister," Rocco said.

Molly laughed. "Say it again, Ben. Not like the insect girl a-tall! By the way, you don't play tennis, do you?"

He shook his head.

"Never mind," Molly said. "I'll teach you as soon as it's warm enough to play on the court. Meanwhile, I've got to practice inside."

"This is going to be Rocco's room," Peggy said.

"Wouldn't you know it," replied Molly. "I guess that means I'm on the way out. If this castle were mine, I'd put in a gym."

"You could use the nursery upstairs," Peggy suggested.

"Where've you been?" said Molly. "Frederick the Great has taken it over."

"What would Freddy be doing up there?"

"Sending messages," Molly said in a low tone. "Beeps in the night. Secret codes. Hush-hush."

"Be serious," Peggy told her.

But Molly was already heading down the hallway. "You'll find out, scout," she called over her shoulder.

Peggy turned to Rocco. "I should apologize for Molly's behavior," she said.

"No, no," he said. "I understand. She is an American girl, right?"

"Well, of course, but—"

He shrugged. "All American girls are wild."

Peggy frowned. "Well, Nell and I are American girls too."

"Yes, see," he said. "You are not married, am I right?"

"No, I am not."

"And yet you travel on train with only your sister. No *scorta*."

"A chaperone? No, it isn't necessary for a chaperone to accompany us."

He smiled and shook his head. "In Italy this would not be allowed."

"We're not in Italy," Peggy said.

Rocco's face broke into a big smile. "Of course not. This is America." He pointed down the hall in the direction Molly had gone. "I like her. She going to teach me the tennis."

Peggy glanced at Nell. "I think he'll fit right in," Nell said helpfully. She liked Rocco a lot already.

"Leave your coat and hat here," Peggy told Rocco. "We might as well take you upstairs to see Freddy. He's a year older than you, but you should fit into his old clothes, if need be."

The nursery was a very large room that occupied most of the third floor. All of the Aldrich children had used it when they were very young. Annie, the family nursemaid, had lovingly watched over them here. Some of their toys—hobby-horses, blocks, doll-houses, windup mechanical animals, and a variety of rubber balls and wooden hoops— were now pushed into a corner. Little trundle beds had been provided for the children to take their naps.

One section of the room had been equipped with small desks and a blackboard. There, Great-aunt Zena had taught the children before they went off to school. The room hadn't really been used much since Nell, the youngest, started going to the village school.

But now, as they reached the top of the staircase, they heard more strange noises. Clicks and squeals that didn't sound as if a person made them. "Maybe Molly has been storing her flies up here?" Nell suggested.

"Not unless she's caught a pig or two as well," said Peggy.

Rocco pointed toward the floor. Thick black wires ran underneath the door. They led across the hallway and out a window. Peggy opened the door cautiously.

Inside, his back to them, sat a chubby boy with straight brown hair that looked as if it hadn't been combed in days. He was wearing a pair of what seemed to be metal earmuffs. In front of him was a black box with silver knobs. The box was where the wires came from.

"Freddy?" called Peggy. He couldn't hear her, no doubt because of the earmuffs. She took a step forward and lifted them off his head.

He turned. "Oh, Peggy," he said. "I was just talking to a friend of mine."

"That's nice," she said. "Where is he? Downstairs?"

"No, he lives in a lighthouse off Nantucket Island."

"Oh. Have they installed a telephone up here?"

Freddy laughed. "No, this is a wireless radio set. I got my license last week. I had to learn Morse code."

"I see," said Peggy. She took Rocco by the arm and introduced him. "Rocco will be staying in the

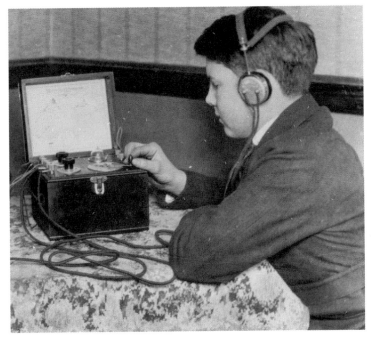

Freddy

room next to yours, and I hoped you could lend him some clothes."

"Rocco?" Freddy said. "Is that an Italian name?"

"*Sì*, yes," Rocco said, pleased.

"It was an Italian who invented the wireless radio," said Freddy.

Rocco nodded. "Marconi," he said. "A great man."

"Oh, this is wonderful," Freddy said. "Are you staying long? I hope so."

Rocco turned to Peggy, letting her answer the question.

"We'll see what Father thinks," she said.

FOUR

What Was in the Bag

ROCCO AWOKE AND FOR A SECOND HE THOUGHT he was still dreaming. Never in his life had he awakened in a room alone. And such a room! Such a bed! Soft, with sheets so clean and white that he barely dared to lie on them. At the window, curtains made of cloth so thin that the sun shone through. Walls decorated with long strips of paper in beautiful designs. So many wonderful things, like a palace, and yet the people who lived here hardly seemed to notice them.

He had never met anyone like these people. Back in Italy, he had imagined that all Americans must be like the Aldrich family. But when he arrived here, he found Americans who were not like that at all. Americans had looked at him suspiciously, as if he had been a thief. In the mill, Americans who were bosses told him he was lazy, slow, stupid. They were not kind at all. They were like the *padrones* in Italy who owned the land.

But the Aldriches were . . . as free and generous as anybody Rocco had ever met. They seemed to do whatever they pleased. If an idea came into their heads, they did not turn it over and over, trying to see what advantage it might hold for them. They just did what they felt like.

The young woman named Peggy had bought him clothes and asked for nothing in return. She brought him to this marvelous home and treated him as a guest. The cousin—the wild one—wanted to play tennis with him. Even the parents were kind and generous. When Rocco had finally met them, they welcomed him and let him share their dinner. A dinner finer than any he had eaten in his whole life!

Had it only been yesterday when fortune smiled upon him? He remembered lying in the alley when an angel found him. A lucky angel who had been born, like him, in the first minute of the century.

His mother had told him that he would be lucky because of that. He had not believed her, for what had ever been lucky in his life? Every day he could remember, he had been hungry. He had seen his three sisters die because they didn't have enough to eat. Late at night, he heard his parents talking. They knew there was no future, no life for them, in Italy.

So one day his father left for America. He promised that when he had earned enough money, he would send for Mama and Rocco. But weeks went by, months, and there was no letter, no money, no ship tickets. Rocco worked for a farmer, who had only a little more to eat than they did. His mother sewed clothing, sometimes working only by the moonlight that came through the window. They could not afford candles.

And then, long after they had given up all hope, a letter came. It was written by a friend of his father's, for his father could not write. The friend said that his father was living in a town called Chicago. Rocco and his mother were to use the ship tickets in the letter to cross the ocean to New York. There, someone would meet them and take them to Chicago.

And so they had gone to Palermo and boarded the ship. It was the first time Rocco had ever seen the ocean. So blue! So big! Impossible to think of sailing across it!

Rocco sat up in bed now, frightened. He closed his eyes and made himself forget the rest of the journey. For whenever he remembered, it made it all happen again. He hoped that if only he could keep it out of his mind, it would go away. All but the last thing his mother had told him. "You are a good boy, Rocco."

He got out of bed. It was time to be a good boy here. For some reason, he had been lucky, and he had learned that it was wise not to waste luck. His new clothes were too fine for work. He put on the pants and shirt and sweater that Freddy had given him last night. Even these old clothes were better than anything Rocco had ever worn.

Downstairs, the Irish woman named Bridget was making coffee in the kitchen. "Well, you're up early!" she said. "I guess you're hungry. I can give you hot or cold cereal, toast or muffins with butter, honey, or preserves, eggs, bacon, and sausage. Milk or tea, if you'd like."

He took a deep breath, nodded, and smiled. The list confused him.

"Well?" she said. "Which is it?"

"Oh, all of those," he replied. "But I like coffee too."

She gave him a funny look. He'd made another mistake, he realized. It was hard to tell what to say. He understood most of the English words, but people acted so differently here. Maybe she didn't think he should be eating before the family was awake. But she had offered him the food, hadn't she?

It made no sense. He wandered into in the dining room, but didn't feel like sitting all by himself at the big table. So he went back to the kitchen and sat on a plain wooden chair next to a table covered with a calico oilcloth. Bridget put a cup of coffee in front of him, along with a pitcher of cream and a bowl of sugar. He didn't like those things in his coffee, but maybe it would be impolite not to take some. So he did.

She brought him a bowl of dry, crunchy flakes with milk to pour into it. He hadn't eaten these before, and the milk didn't make them taste much better. Then came hot cereal, with some maple syrup poured on top of it. That was very good tasting. And then she brought fried eggs, and some more—and some more—

He figured out his mistake about the time she finished cooking the bacon and started on sausages. By then, it was too late to tell Bridget to stop, that he'd had enough. The look on her face showed that she'd decided it was a contest. She was going to see if he really could eat everything she cooked.

Rocco spread some raspberry preserves on the bacon and put it between two pieces of buttered toast. The look on Bridget's face showed him that was a mistake too. But on the train they'd served him bacon on a burnt bread sandwich.

He sighed as she set a plate of sausages in front of him. "Too much for you?" Bridget asked.

"No, no," he said. "I am just enjoying how well you cook."

She darted a suspicious look at him. "Not going to put preserves on the sausages, are you?"

He thought about it. "Not if it is not proper."

Her face softened a little. "Well, most people wouldn't do it," she said.

Rocco nodded. "I thank you." He speared a sausage with his fork and bit into it. It was delicious. He almost cried because he couldn't hold any more.

"You really didn't want all that food, did you?" said Bridget.

"I like very much," he insisted.

She watched him. He took another sausage from the plate. "Michael told me you're from Italy," Bridget said.

He nodded, chewing slowly.

"I remember how it was in Ireland before I came here," she said. "People were starving. They dropped right down in the fields, digging with their hands for a potato."

He swallowed, and took another bite.

"That must be how it is in Italy," she said.

He looked at the last sausage, and thought of his sisters. Tears came to his eyes, surprising him. So strange, so strange to think that in America people would feed him food until he could eat no more.

"I have had enough," he said.

He started to get to his feet, but found standing up was more difficult than usual. Holding onto the edge of the table, he managed it.

"You should go out for a nice walk," said Bridget. "Tramp around and work off some of that meal."

Rocco slipped on a woolen pullover that hung by the door. Outside, the cold air struck him like a fist. Although he had been in America for more than two years, he had never gotten used to the winters. At least there were only a few patches of snow on the ground right now. The day was sunny and clear.

He followed a path that led around the house. Smoke wafted from the twin chimneys high above. A crow cawed at him from a tree bare of leaves. Rocco noticed flower beds all along the sides of the house. Although the cold had killed the tops of the plants, he could see that in summer the beds had been overgrown by weeds. Nobody had bothered to pull them.

Someone called his name. He looked up. A window on the second floor was open, and Freddy stuck his head out. "What are you doing up so early?" he called.

"Could not sleep," Rocco called back. He was going to say, "I was hungry," but changed his mind. Someone might bring him more food.

"You want to go ice skating?" said Freddy.

Rocco shook his head. He wanted to walk alone and think. For the past two years, he hardly had any time to do such simple things. But this family, these Aldriches, seemed always to want to be doing something.

"Stay there! I'll be right down," Freddy called.

Rocco waited, kicking at the frozen ground. He expected that one of the girls would appear soon, wanting to play tennis or teach him to ride a bicycle.

Freddy appeared, out of breath and still buttoning his coat. "You no have a breakfast?" asked Rocco.

"No, I don't have breakfast because I eat late at night," Freddy said. "When I'm listening to the messages from ships at sea. They come in clearer at night. I'll teach you."

"I no want to hear ships," said Rocco firmly.

"Oh, you must," said Freddy.

Rocco pointed at the ground. "Somebody planted flowers here?"

"I guess so," Freddy replied. "Grandma and Aunt Zena used to garden, but since Grandma died . . . "

"Where they keep the tools?" asked Rocco.

"Oh, you can't garden now," Freddy told him. "The ground is frozen. See?" He stamped on the earth as if Rocco were an idiot and could not see. "It's too hard."

"You must start some things early," Rocco replied. "Inside the house."

Freddy scratched his head. "Well, there's a shed where Michael keeps things." He showed Rocco where it was.

Rocco was excited. A look inside showed that everything he wanted was there. He found some small clay pots, trowels, and a tray. In the corner stood a bag filled with dark rich loam. Rocco ran his fingers through the crumbly, musty earth. It brought back memories, and he closed his eyes.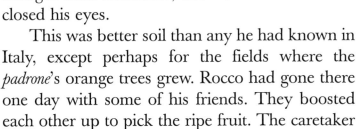

This was better soil than any he had known in Italy, except perhaps for the fields where the *padrone*'s orange trees grew. Rocco had gone there one day with some of his friends. They boosted each other up to pick the ripe fruit. The caretaker had fired a shotgun at them, from far away. Rocco remembered the juice running down his chin as he fled.

"You're getting your hands dirty," Freddy said.

Rocco opened his eyes, and the sunny fields disappeared. "Yes," he said. He took some of the clay pots and scooped soil from the bag.

"If we go skating now, we'll have the lake all to ourselves," Freddy said encouragingly.

Rocco put the pots inside a tray and carried them outside. Freddy followed as Rocco walked toward the house. "Where are you going to put those?" Freddy asked.

"Next to the window in my room," Rocco answered. "The sun shines through there in the morning."

"I'm not sure that's a good idea," said Freddy. "Bridget tries to keep the house very clean. She doesn't like Uncle Georgie to come inside at all."

"I saw the plants growing in the downstairs rooms," said Rocco.

Freddy thought. "Oh, yes. But those are tropical plants. Ferns, and those tall things with all the leaves."

"They are fig trees," said Rocco. "They will grow anywhere."

"Really? Well, anyway . . . what kind of plants could you grow in your room? And where would you get them?"

Rocco stopped at the back door because his hands were full. Freddy stepped around him to open it.

Bridget's back was turned, and she didn't see them as they slipped through the hallway. They made their way up the back stairs and down the hallway. Freddy opened the door to Rocco's room, and they went inside.

Freddy sat down on the bed, curious to see what would happen.

Rocco sighed. If only the Aldriches weren't so friendly and so nice. He went to the closet and took the old leather bag from his overcoat. He reached inside and pulled out a folded-up piece of brown paper.

Unwrapping it, he explained, "These are seeds that my mother brought from Italy." He showed Freddy the small dried yellow specks.

"What kind of seeds are they?"

"Tomatoes and basil and oregano. The tomatoes need a long time to grow, so you must start them early." He put a seed into each of the clay pots, carefully poking it into the soil with his finger.

"We can buy tomatoes from the local farmers in the summertime," said Freddy.

"Not like these," replied Rocco. "You will see."

FIVE

Do Women Want to Vote?

"HAVE YOU SEEN ROCCO?" NELL ASKED BRIDGET.

"He's outside rolling in the mud, as usual," came the reply.

He wasn't really, of course. Bridget was a little crabby because Rocco had been tracking dirt into the house. He taken over the job of tending the gardens. Nobody thought there was much for him to do, because here in Maine the ground was still mostly frozen.

But Rocco was getting ready for spring. Every day now, he went out to clean up the debris left by last year's plants and to plan this year's gardens. Some seed catalogs addressed to Grandma still arrived each year, and Rocco had found them. He

was surprised by the idea that you could get flower and vegetable seeds and plants by mail.

Mama and Aunt Maud looked at the catalogs and told Rocco to order some. When Great-aunt Zena heard what was going on, she decided to supervise. That was when she found out Rocco couldn't read. Great-aunt Zena couldn't get up the stairs to the third-floor classroom any longer. So she gave Rocco lessons for an hour each day in the solarium. Because that room was so sunny, they decided to start the new seeds in there.

But Rocco still kept his own seeds in pots on his bedroom windowsill. Nell had seen them sprouting. When she asked about them, he didn't say very much, just that they were tomatoes and herbs. But Freddy told Nell that Rocco had kept the seeds in his leather bag. "He brought them from Italy," he said.

Nell was curious about him. He was always polite, but he never really said anything about himself. Even so, he made friends with everybody. Even Bridget and Great-aunt Zena liked him—sort of. When they criticized him, they did it in a mild way.

Nell's mother even said, "Your friend Rocco has awakened Aunt Zena."

"What do you mean?"

"She hasn't taken an interest in anything since your grandmother died," said Mother. "Now, she and Rocco are planning gardens and she's teaching him to read. I haven't seen her so active in a long time."

And today, as Nell went outside in search of Rocco, she saw Great-aunt Zena standing over him. Rocco was putting wooden stakes into the ground and connecting them with pieces of string. Zena was directing the work, pointing here and there with her cane.

When Nell reached them, she said, "Oh, Aunt Zena, do you think Rocco can go to Kennebunk with us?"

"Certainly not," said Aunt Zena. "There's too much work to be done."

"Peggy's going to meet a college chum who is coming to visit," Nell said. "There's room in the car for Rocco and we thought he'd enjoy the drive."

Rocco turned and smiled at her. "Thank you," he said. "But your aunt is right. We are getting ready to plant soon."

Nell nodded and went around to the front of the house, where Peggy was already waiting in the car with Michael. They were arguing, because Peggy wanted to drive.

"I'll have none of that," said Michael. "If you take over my job, then there's no work for me, and I might as well go back to Ireland."

"You can find something else to do around here today," said Peggy. "Rocco is helping with the gardens."

"Oh, he is. Well, I'm not one to traipse in the mud like a pig rooting for acorns."

"I guess that's not good enough for you."

"It's not what I've been hired to do. One thing I'm supposed to do is watch out for you and your sister. Now get in."

Nell could hear Peggy grind her teeth as she climbed into the back seat. Peggy didn't think anybody needed to watch over her.

As the car started down the driveway, Peggy muttered, "Someday, I will be in charge of Aldrich house, and things will change."

Nell wondered if that were true. Grandfather had left the house, along with the theater he'd built by the lake, to his four children—Richard, William, Maud, and Georgie. He wanted them to continue the tradition of presenting plays free on a holiday. Of course, there was room enough in the house for everyone, but some members of the family were usually somewhere else. Uncle Richard and Aunt Laura, for instance, were in Great Britain performing Shakespeare.

Peggy and Nell and their parents lived here, because Papa had taken over the job of managing the estate. Aunt Maud, the mother of Freddy and the twins, was usually here too. But her husband, Uncle Nick, was in New York right now, acting in a comedy called *Green Stockings*. Uncle Georgie, the youngest, was sort of an inventor. But right now he was taking flying lessons in Massachusetts.

It seemed to Nell that it would be a long time before Peggy would be one of the owners of the house. Anyway, she'd have to share it with Nell and their cousins. The only thing that Grandfather had left Peggy was his big old pocket watch. She kept it in her room, but Nell had heard it play a tune when the cover was open. Peggy would not say why she never let the cover stay open long enough to hear the song finish.

Peggy leaned over the front seat of the car. "Stop at the general store in town," she said. "I want to buy some thread."

That was a surprise. "What do you need thread for?" Nell asked. "Aunt Maud has plenty of it you can use anytime."

Peggy's only response was a glare. Nell sat back. She decided that Peggy just wanted to order Michael to do something.

He eased the car to a stop in front of the store. POMEROY'S EMPORIUM, read the sign. Next door was the POMEROY MOVIE THEATER. The Aldriches tried not to shop at the store if they could help it. There had been bad feelings between the Aldriches and the Pomeroys for a long time.

But as soon as they went inside, Marshall Pomeroy gave them a big smile from behind the counter. Marshall's father had been elected mayor a few years ago, so Marshall ran the store and movie theater now.

His black hair was slicked down so smooth that it looked painted on. His face was red and thin. Along with the red-and-white striped shirt he wore under a pair of red suspenders, he looked like the top of a candy cane.

"If it isn't Peggy Aldrich," he said. "I don't see you often enough."

"Your stock isn't usually the quality I need," Peggy said coldly.

"Is that so?" For some reason, Peggy's remark didn't seem to dent his smile. "Well, make sure you take one of these handbills before you go. I've been distributing them all week." He pointed to a stack of papers on the store counter. Nell walked over and read the top one.

Peggy picked up one of the handbills and read it too. "This is complete nonsense," she said to Marshall. "Anyway, you're a bit late. The women's suffrage proposal has already been voted down in Maine."

"Yes, but some people won't take no for an answer," Marshall said. "Now there's a move to

Some Reasons
WHY SOME WOMEN
O P P O S E
votes for
WOMEN

- The great advances for women in the last century have been made without women having the power to vote.

- The basis of government is physical force. The law must be enforced by physical power. That is neither possible nor desirable for women.

- Women are able to achieve greater influence because they belong to no political party. Thus, they can appeal to both parties for help.

- The demand for women's suffrage is made by a small minority of women. The majority of women would rather not have the power to vote.

ask Congress for a constitutional amendment to let women vote. My father says we've got to keep fighting to keep them out of politics and at home where they belong."

"Does he indeed?" Peggy said. "I guess that's because people like him would be swept out of office if women could vote."

"Not at all," Marshall replied. "Every decent woman in town approves of the job he's doing."

"Well, I'm glad you showed me this, Marshall," said Peggy. "I was discouraged by the results of the vote last year. But now I see that someone must explain why women need to vote—right here in Lake Chohobee!"

Peggy turned and swept out of the store. Nell followed, thinking it wouldn't be a good idea to remind Peggy that they hadn't bought the thread.

Michael noticed though. "You weren't in there very long," he said as the car started down the road again.

Peggy pursed her lips and didn't reply.

"Is that Marshall Pomeroy just as pleasant a lad as ever?" Michael asked with a smile.

"Worse," Peggy mumbled.

The drive down to Kennebunk didn't take long, and the train hadn't arrived yet. "I've told you about Harriet Porter. She was one of my roommates my last two years in college," Peggy told Nell. "She and I first met in the women's suffrage club.

You'll find her an interesting person. Her father's quite wealthy but you wouldn't know it."

The train arrived, and Peggy scanned the faces of the passengers getting off. All at once, she waved and cried out. Nell saw a young woman wave back. She had red hair that was tied up in a bun and wore a green dress with matching jacket. It was true that she had a casual look about her, but Nell thought the dress looked expensive.

A porter brought Harriet's luggage—two suitcases, a hatbox, an overnight case, and a cardboard box that bore the name of a fashionable New York store. Michael stowed them in the trunk of the car.

"Can you imagine that it's been almost a year since we've graduated?" said Harriet. "What have you been doing?"

Harriet

"Taking photographs, mostly," Peggy replied.

"Photographs? How modern a thing to be doing. I tried to paint for a while, but I'm hopeless. I can't even paint a cloud."

"You should be writing," Peggy told her. "You could always write so well."

"For the college newspaper, yes," Harriet replied. "But my father wouldn't let me write for a regular newspaper. He knows the publisher of *The*

New York Times, too. But he thinks a newspaper office isn't a proper place for a girl." She giggled. "To tell you the truth, he has a husband picked out for me."

"That's terrible," said Peggy. "Who is it?"

"Oh, some boy," replied Harriet with a wave of her hand. "He's just the sort of person my father would think is right for his daughter. I suppose I will marry him eventually, but I want to *create* something first. Can I tell you a secret?" she asked with sparkling eyes.

"Of course," Peggy said.

Harriet looked at Nell. "*I* won't tell anybody," Nell said.

"It's all right," said Harriet. "That's the reason I came up for a visit. Of course, to see you. You know that. But I know your family has its annual theater production in the summer. You still do, don't you?"

"Oh, yes," said Peggy.

"Well, I thought I'd try my hand at writing a play."

Peggy blinked. "A play? You mean . . . *our* play?"

"Well, your family would be the actors, of course. I wouldn't go on the stage to save my life, I'm afraid. But my father couldn't have any objections to my *writing* a play. He wouldn't have to know until afterward. I'd invite all my friends to come see it, of course."

Nell could see that Peggy had some doubts about the idea. "What would the play be about?" she asked Harriet. "Have you anything . . . ?"

"Oh, yes," said Harriet. "I think it should illustrate the importance of contact with the spirit world."

The Ouija Board Speaks

"I DIDN'T *KNOW*," PEGGY WAS EXPLAINING. NELL thought she was wasting her breath. Mother and Aunt Maud didn't seem concerned by the news that Harriet wanted to take over their summer theater production. Peggy herself was the one who was most upset.

The four of them were in the downstairs parlor. Harriet had gone upstairs to unpack and freshen up. "She'll become bored and go back to New York before long," said Mother. "Life here is not as exciting as in the big city."

But it turned out that Harriet had brought some excitement with her. After dinner, the family

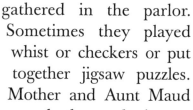

gathered in the parlor. Sometimes they played whist or checkers or put together jigsaw puzzles. Mother and Aunt Maud were both good singers, and practically everyone knew how to play the small piano that stood against the wall. They also had a Gramophone with some recordings that Aunt Laura had made. Often, they put a recording on and sang along.

However, Harriet promptly announced that she had brought a Ouija board.

Nell had never heard of such a thing. Looking around the room she could see that most of the others hadn't either. "Isn't that a fortune-telling device?" Papa asked.

"Oh, it's nothing so common as that," Harriet proclaimed. "A Ouija board works on scientific principles. It channels the thoughts of spirits into a material form."

"What scientific principles?" asked Polly.

"The ones discovered by Madame Blavatsky," replied Harriet.

"Oh," said Polly. "I've never heard of her."

"Twenty years ago, people never heard of radio waves, either," said Harriet. "But today everyone believes in them."

"I have a radio set upstairs," said Freddy. "But you need another radio set to send messages. Do the spirits have Ouija boards too?"

"It's not like that," said Harriet. "The spirits are all around us right at this very moment."

Everybody sort of glanced around the room. Nell felt foolish, but the way Harriet said it made her think it must be true.

"The Ouija is very simple to use," said Harriet. She placed the Ouija board on the table where the family usually played cards. Nell went over to look. On top of it were printed all the letters of the alphabet, plus the numbers 0 through 9. The words YES and NO were below these.

Then Harriet put a small triangle-shaped object on top of the board. Nell could see that underneath each corner was a small wheel. "This is the planchette," said Harriet, keeping her hand on the wooden triangle so it wouldn't slide away.

"I need two volunteers," said Harriet. Nell shyly raised her hand.

"That's one. How about you?" Harriet asked, pointing to Polly.

Polly shook her head. "I'd rather observe," she said.

Her twin Molly stepped forward. "I'll give it a spin, Min," she said.

"Now each of us will place a finger on each of the corners of the planchette," said Harriet. Nell and Polly both reached for the same corner, and

then giggled as their hands met. Harriet frowned. "You must be serious," she said. "The spirits will not speak to us otherwise."

Nell avoided looking at Polly so she wouldn't be tempted to laugh again. She put her finger on the planchette. "Now everyone concentrate," said Harriet. "Think of someone you know who has departed this world."

Nell wondered who she should think about. She remembered Grandma a little, but not much about Grandpa. Peggy loved Grandpa a lot, and—

She looked down. The planchette had started to move. It was a strange feeling, as if her finger were being carried along. Then it stopped, right under the letter L on the Ouija board.

"L," Harriet announced. "Has anyone been thinking of a person whose name begins with L?"

"Lionel." Several people—Mama, Papa, Aunt Maud, and Peggy—said it at the same time.

Lionel was Grandpa's first name.

Papa spoke up, a little too loudly. "Well, if Father is here, I wouldn't be surprised. He loved this house."

"Would anyone like to ask him something?" asked Harriet.

No one responded for a moment. Then Nell said, "I would. Is it all right?"

"Of course," said Harriet.

"I want to ask if he'd like the summer play to be about spiritualism."

Harriet raised her eyebrows and gave Nell a look. "All right," she said. "We can ask that." She raised her voice. "Lionel! We would like to know if you wish us to write a play about those who seek knowledge of the spirit world."

Papa

All at once, Nell felt the planchette move. She wasn't sure, but she felt as if Harriet were guiding it. It seemed to be headed for the word YES. Nell concentrated, and found that by pressing downward, she could move the planchette in the opposite direction. It was hard though.

Then the planchette definitely started to move toward the word NO. Nell glanced over and saw

Molly wink at her. But the planchette slowed down before it could get there. It came to a stop in the middle of the board.

"The answer is unclear," Harriet said. She put a hand to her forehead. "I sense confusion in the room. It has disturbed the spirits." She looked around.

"You," she said, pointing to Rocco. He was sitting quietly near the doorway. He looked around, hoping she meant someone else.

"Come here," she said. "What's your name?" Everybody had been introduced earlier, but Harriet had forgotten.

"Rocco," he told her softly.

"I sense that you have a deep sympathy with the spirits," she said.

By now everybody was looking at Rocco. His face reddened.

He wouldn't budge until Harriet walked over and took his arm. She led him to the table where the Ouija board was. She brushed Nell and Molly out of the way. "Now you and I will try to let the spirits speak to us, Rocco. You understand?"

He nodded, but Nell could see that he was uncomfortable. As Harriet showed Rocco how to place his finger on the planchette, Nell put hers on the third corner.

Harriet looked annoyed. "Is there anyone else who'd like to try?" she called out.

But nobody volunteered, and Nell stood where she was. She gave Rocco a smile to reassure him. It didn't help.

"Rocco," said Harriet, "is there anyone among the spirits you wish to speak to?" she asked.

He pressed his lips together and nodded.

"Who is it?" she asked.

"*Mia madre*," he said, in such a low voice that Nell hardly heard.

"Your mother?" Harriet nodded confidently. "What would you like to ask her?"

Rocco swallowed. It was hard for him to speak. "*Dove padre?*" he said finally.

"*Dove padre?*" Harriet didn't understand. She looked around the room.

Peggy spoke up. "He is asking where his father is," she said. "I think you should stop now, Harriet."

"Oh, no," Harriet said. "This is very interesting. Say it again, Rocco." She looked at Nell and said, "And this time, try to be more receptive."

Rocco took a deep breath. Nell wanted to help him, but didn't know how. "*Dove padre?*" he said, more firmly than before.

Nell felt the planchette start to move. She wasn't doing anything to help it along. It seemed to know just where to go, and stopped at the letter D.

"D," Harriet announced. She closed her eyes. "I think the message has more to it."

The planchette moved a few letters to the left.

"A," said Harriet.

Nell glanced at Rocco. He stared down at the board as if snakes were crawling on it. The planchette moved again, and Nell was sure Rocco wasn't moving it.

Harriet continued to read off the letters where the planchette stopped. "N . . . G . . . R."

Nell felt the force that was guiding the planchette weaken. The triangle went back to the middle of the Ouija board and rested there.

"That is all," said Harriet. "D . . . A . . . N . . . G . . . R," she repeated.

"Danger!" someone said softly. Nell turned her head. It was Freddy, standing next to the fireplace. His eyes were wide, as if he felt the danger himself.

Harriet nodded, and turned to Rocco. "Your father may be in danger," she said.

"There wasn't any E in the word," Papa said from his seat on the far side of the room. "Perhaps the message meant something else."

"Such as what?" said Harriet.

Before Papa could answer, Rocco turned and ran out of the room. They could hear his footsteps going up the staircase.

Nell couldn't contain herself any longer. "You've upset him," she said to Harriet. "I think that was cruel."

"The answer came from the spirits," Harriet said. "I only served as a messenger."

Nell shook her head angrily and went after Rocco.

Upstairs, the door to his room was closed. Nell hesitated, and then knocked quietly. Almost at once, it opened. Rocco was there, wearing his overcoat and cap.

"Where are you going?" asked Nell.

He shrugged. "I think maybe I should go find work to do."

Nell was shocked. "Why would you do that?"

"I have stayed here too long," he said. "I do not belong here."

"Why, that's not true," she told him. "Everybody wants you to stay. What would happen to your plants?"

He turned to let her see into the room. He had been wrapping the pots in some old newspapers. "I can take them with me," he said. "I would return the pots later. I would not steal them."

"That's ridiculous. You shouldn't be that upset over Harriet's silly Ouija board. She didn't mean to frighten you."

He shook his head. "I was not frighten. I saw she was making fun with me. The Ouija is a . . . trick. One of those things that people use to fool you with."

"I thought so too," said Nell. "How did you know?"

"When Harriet told me to ask my mother a question—" He trailed off and stopped.

"Yes?"

"I thought for a moment maybe my mother would answer."

"Well, we did get an answer."

"Yes, but what was the answer?" he asked.

"According to Harriet, it was 'danger.'"

Rocco spread his hands. "That could not have been what my mother say."

Nell was puzzled. "Why not? There might really be danger from something."

"Oh, danger, yes. But see, my mother, she only spoke Italian. If she wanted to warn me, she would say, 'Rocco, *guardarsi*.' She would not have used an English word."

Nell laughed, and then put her hand over her mouth. "Please don't be offended," she said. "I just thought that was clever of you."

"Truly?" he asked. "But this Harriet think I am enough stupid to believe her trick."

"No, she's just foolish," said Nell. "Please take off your coat. All of us would be very upset if you left."

He looked at her for a second, and then decided she was sincere. He took off the coat and hat and put them in the closet. Nell helped him unwrap the pots.

"Rocco," she said. "I want to ask you something."

"Yes, ask," he said.

"You don't have to answer."

"All right."

"Why did you ask your mother where your father is?"

He sighed and sat down on the bed. "In Italy," he said quietly, "I had three sisters. They all died. We buried them, each one, in the cemetery by the church." He closed his eyes, and Nell knew that he was remembering.

After a moment, he went on. "When we decided to come to America, I thought my mother would not be able to leave my sisters. She had gone to visit their graves each Sunday. Because maybe . . . we would never return. When we were getting ready to leave, I asked my mother what about this. And she told me, 'I will bring them with me in my heart.'"

Nell couldn't speak. It was such a sad story she didn't know what to say.

Then Rocco looked up at her, his large brown eyes shining. "The answer to your question I have in my heart now. I thought maybe I would never let it out, but you have been a good friend to me."

He went to the closet and brought out the small leather sack. He took out an envelope and showed it to her. Inside was a piece of paper that looked as if it had been handled many times.

"This is the letter my father had someone write to us after he go to America," said Rocco.

"There were ship tickets inside. My father could not write it himself. And my mother could not read it, so she took it to our village priest, who read it to us. It says that when we use the tickets to cross the ocean, someone will be waiting to meet us. Only *mi madre* . . . on the boat, she got sick. She die. And when I arrived alone in New York, no one was there to meet me."

"What did you do?" Nell asked. "I would have been terrified."

Rocco nodded. "You think I was not afraid? With all those people in that building at Ellis Island? They poked me, looked into my eyes, and my mouth, and my ears. Asked me questions. On the ship, a man had told me to say I had five dollars. You have to have five dollars to get into America, he tell me. Even though we were coming because we were poor. But maybe they ask me to show the five dollars. Where would I get five dollars? You know where?"

Nell shook her head.

"This man stayed with me when we got off the ship. After he passed the examination, he came around in back of the line and gave me his five dollars. Then after they passed me through, I returned it."

Nell laughed.

"Yes, right," said Rocco. "A trick. So then later this man saw me waiting and said did I want a job?

Ellis Island

And I thought that I had better have a job. So we came up to Lawrence, Massachusetts, and I got my job."

"You should have waited until your father's friend got there," Nell said.

Rocco shook his head. "I waited all day. At night they make you leave or put you in jail. The only other thing was to go on the boat back to Italy. I had no money for a ticket. So what could I do?"

"Let me see the letter," said Nell.

She examined the envelope and then took out the thin sheet of paper that was inside. Of course it was written in Italian. "There's a return address," she said. "It's in Chicago. Can I show this to Mama and Papa?"

Rocco hesitated. "You don't think they would want me to leave?"

"No, of course not. But they might be able to find the man who wrote it."

He shrugged. "I guess it will be all right."

"And as for Harriet . . . don't let her bother you. We'll do something about her, too."

Rocco was surprised at the way Nell sounded. "What are you going to do?" he asked.

"I have an idea," she replied.

The Sailor's Ghost

APRIL 5–8, 1912

NELL DIDN'T LOSE ANY TIME PUTTING HER PLAN into action. She went downstairs and peeked into the parlor. Harriet was still trying to persuade people to use the Ouija board. Nell caught Molly's eye from the doorway and pointed toward the kitchen.

In a few minutes, Molly joined her there. "What's up, Pup?" she asked.

"Do you know where Polly keeps the flies she catches?"

"Whoa," replied Molly. "You've got the wrong twin. I thought you could tell us apart."

"I can. You're the one with the bump on your nose."

"Broke it falling out of a tree, and you're the only one who knows it." Nell had been watching when Molly broke her nose and promised to keep it a secret. She always had.

"Why do you want the flies?" Molly asked.

Nell told her.

Molly burst into laughter. "That should put her in a swivet. All right, they're still down in the root cellar, as far as I know. Shall we get them now?"

They lit a kerosene lantern that Bridget kept in a closet for emergencies. Even so, when they went to the back of the house and opened the trapdoor to the cellar, it looked awfully dark.

Molly sniffed as they carefully went down the steps. "Smells like my sister is raising molds and toadstools down here too. Think she'll turn out to be a witch when she grows up?"

Nell sneezed as a cobweb brushed across her face. "Why does Polly keep them here?"

"I think she hopes they'll die and she won't have to see them," replied Molly. "But she had to move them. She used to keep them where Bridget stores her preserves. One day, Bridget picked up a jar that she thought would be full of peaches. She could feel it wasn't heavy enough, so she opened it up. Guess what flew out? Well, she raised a fuss, Gus."

"I remember," Nell said.

"Do you really believe that flies carry these germ things around and make people sick?" asked Molly.

"That's what scientists say," replied Nell.

"I wonder why God made something so small we can't see it."

"Peggy said she saw germs through a microscope at college."

"Maybe, but to me that's cheating."

Molly lifted the lantern and they saw the wooden door to the room that was used for storing roots. These were vegetables that could be eaten all winter, like carrots, turnips, parsnips, and potatoes. Molly raised the latch and the door swung open. They saw a dozen large glass canning jars sitting neatly on a shelf.

"They might already be dead," said Molly.

"I think they sort of hibernate when it's cold," Nell told her. "Pick up a jar and let's take a look." She hated to admit it, but she didn't want to touch the jars herself.

Molly lifted a jar and held it next to the lantern. There were some flies on the bottom of it, but as the lantern heated the jar, they flapped their wings. "This bunch is ready to fly," said Molly. "How many jars do you think we'll need?"

"I was hoping they'd be noisier," said Nell.

"We can fix that," Molly told her. "Let's take a few jars upstairs. Can you carry two?"

"I guess," said Nell. She told herself it was for a good cause. Anyway, the flies couldn't get out. She hoped.

Gingerly, the girls brought four jars up to Molly's room without anyone noticing. "They're a bit more lively," Molly commented. "Hardly any of them seem dead."

"But they aren't as noisy as I hoped," said Nell.

"It's because the jar lids are too tight," replied Molly. "I have something that will fix it." She rummaged in a bureau drawer and brought out some rice paper. "This was for wrapping presents, but I can't get the hang of it," she said.

She cut off a square of paper. Carefully she screwed the lid off one of the jars, and slipped the square over the top. Then she held it in place with a rubber band and shook the jar. The paper made the flies' buzzing sound much louder.

Nell clapped her hands. "That's just the effect I wanted."

In a few minutes, they had replaced all the jar lids. "Now's the hard part," said Molly. "Where'll we put 'em?"

"Some place where she can hear them—but not find them," Nell replied. "Not under her bed or anyplace she can easily get to."

"Did Peggy ever show you how you can hear what's going on downstairs by listening at the air vents?"

Nell shook her head.

"No? What kind of sister *is* she?" Molly commented. "Well, you can. The vents run all through the house. Now let's see . . . which room is Harriet staying in?"

They found a small storeroom on the third floor that was directly over Harriet's room. Using the lantern, they found the vent that led down to the second floor. They removed the cover and looked down. Dimly, they could see the quilt on Harriet's bed. "We can't just drop the jars," said Nell. "We'll need something to lower them down."

Molly found a ball of string, which they tied to the jars. Carefully, they lowered each one into the hole in the floor. "Sounds good," said Molly. "I can still hear them from up here."

"There's nothing more annoying at night than the sound of a fly," said Nell.

"And fifty of them ought to keep her awake all night," replied Molly. "But maybe she's the type that doesn't need sleep. What then, Ben?"

"Here's the rest of my plan," said Nell.

The next morning, Nell made sure she came downstairs early for breakfast. Even so, Rocco was there before her. Bridget was asking Rocco if he was sure he had enough to eat. "How are you today?" Nell asked him.

He nodded and smiled. "Good," he said. He waited until Bridget left the room, and then asked, "You not tell anybody what I said last night?"

"Oh, no," Nell replied. "But I'm going to show the letter to Father as soon as I get a chance."

"Maybe you should not," he said. "I could get in trouble."

She was puzzled. "I don't see how."

"Because I show someone else's five dollars to get through Ellis Island."

"I see. Well, no one will remember, I'm sure. We just want to find your father, if we can."

One by one, everybody else in the house arrived in the dining room. Harriet was the last one to come downstairs. She looked terrible . . . almost as if she hadn't slept at all.

"Do you feel all right, Harriet?" Mama asked.

"No," she said crossly. Then she recovered her manners. "I'm sorry, but I was completely unable to sleep. There seemed to be a fly in my room. Several flies, in fact."

Mama

Everybody looked down the table at Polly, who was lifting a spoonful of hot oatmeal toward her mouth. Her eyes got very wide. "Well, I'm sure *I* don't know anything about that," she said.

"Er . . . " Nell's father began. "Could some of your flies have gotten into Harriet's room?"

"Oh, no, Uncle William," Polly said. "They're all down in the root cellar . . . freezing to death, I guess." A tear came to her eye.

"Well, then," he replied, "Right after breakfast, why don't you take your net and an empty jar up to Harriet's room? See if you can catch the one that bothered her."

"*Certainly* more than one," Harriet added.

Nell and Molly shot a glance at each other. "I think I'm finished," Nell said suddenly.

"Me too," chimed in Molly. "May we be excused?"

"Of course, girls," said Mama. "It's such a nice day, I'm sure you'll want to go outside."

"Not just yet," Nell called as they headed for the staircase. "We want to, um . . . "

" . . . do some sewing," Molly finished for her.

As they reached the second floor, Molly whispered, "They're *always* happy when we're sewing."

"But how are we going to get the flies back?" asked Nell, as they headed up to the third floor. "We can't reach them from above."

"Let's go to the attic," Molly said. "There's always something you can use up there."

That was true. It was full of steamer trunks that held old costumes. Leaning against the rafters were props and mementos of all the theaters the Aldriches had ever appeared in. And sure enough, the girls found a long pair of metal tongs that looked like they'd once been part of a fireplace set. "You think we could pick up the jars with these?" asked Molly, snapping them open and closed.

"The glass might slip," said Nell. "Let's tie some rags around each end of the tongs."

That did the trick. By the time they were lifting the last jar out of the ventilator shaft, Polly and Harriet walked into the room below. Nell and Molly could see them looking around for the horde of flies that had bothered Harriet.

"Where will we put the flies?" whispered Nell.

"Let's take them to the attic for now," said Polly. "Are we going to bring them back tonight?"

"Yes. I think it will take at least two more nights," replied Nell.

It didn't. At breakfast the next morning, Harriet was haggard. She looked as if she'd spent a week on a desert island. There were dark bags under her eyes and her cheeks seemed sunken. "I don't think I can stay in that room another night," she said.

"I'm terribly sorry," said Mother.

"Really, Aunt Anna, we couldn't find any flies in there yesterday," said Polly.

"Perhaps something else is making the noise," suggested Aunt Maud.

Molly said brightly, "It might be the spirits of the flies Polly has killed."

Everyone frowned at her—except Nell, who stifled a laugh with her napkin.

"We'll have to find you another room," Mother told Harriet. "I'll ask Bridget to put fresh linens in the other guest bedroom."

"I'll be glad to show Harriet where it is," said Nell. "Molly and I can help her move her things down the hall."

"That's very nice of you, dear."

Mother's praise made Nell feel a little guilty. But she reminded herself that if Harriet stayed, the summer would be ruined.

So while she and Molly were watching Harriet pack her lovely peach-colored peignoir, Nell said, "You ought to find your new room very interesting."

"Why is that?" Harriet asked.

"Because it's the most likely place in the house to have spirits."

That was Molly's cue. "Oh, don't tell Harriet about that, Nell. You'll frighten her."

Harriet gave a little laugh. "I assure you, I'm quite at home with the spirits."

"Well, *that's* good," said Nell. She picked up one of Harriet's pale blue silk stockings and put it across her eyes. She could see right through it. "But there's a story about the spirit in that room."

"I can't listen," said Molly, putting her hands to her ears.

"She's right," Nell said, "I shouldn't tell you about it."

"I insist that you tell me," said Harriet firmly.

"It's sort of a family secret."

"I hope you can trust *me*."

"Well, not many people know that our grand-father Lionel had a brother. His name was . . . Tigerel."

Molly rolled her eyes, but she was sitting behind Harriet and only Nell could see her.

"Tigerel?" said Harriet. "I certainly never heard of him."

"Well, you see, he wasn't an actor. He went to sea, traveled all over the world. He saw all kinds of strange people. And while he was in . . . was it Borneo, Molly?"

"I thought it was Mongolia."

"Mongolia has no seacoast," said Harriet.

"Then it must have been Borneo. At any rate, he took this idol that the natives worshipped."

"An *idol?*"

"Yes. A statue."

"And it had two huge eyes made of rubies," said Molly.

Harriet looked at them strangely. "I never heard this story before."

"Well, it's because of what *happened*," said Nell.

"You see," continued Molly, "he sold the rubies. For a fortune. And then he came back here to live. He had enough money to retire."

"He brought the idol with him, and kept it in his room," said Nell.

"The room where you're going to be," Molly pointed out.

"That *is* interesting," said Harriet. "Is it still there?"

"No," Nell went on. She lowered her voice. "Because one night, there was a terrible scream that woke up everybody in the house."

"And when they came to see what happened," said Molly, "they found that the idol had disappeared . . . and Tigerel was dead!"

"But worst of all," said Molly, "his eyes had been plucked out." She opened her own eyes very wide, to show just how awful it must have been.

"Oh!" exclaimed Harriet. "That's a horrible story!"

"It's why nobody talks about it," said Molly.

"And the idol was never found?" asked Harriet.

"Not only that," said Molly, "but people say that Tigerel sometimes comes back, late at night."

"He wants to get his eyes back," said Nell. She could see that Harriet was bothered by the story.

"Well," Harriet said, trying to make light of it, "he'll have to go back to Borneo to get them, won't he?"

"Unless he can get them from someone else," said Molly.

Harriet had no reply to that. She looked like she'd just lost some more sleep. "Why don't you girls go and play?" she said. "I can finish packing myself."

Molly and Nell were glad to leave. They ran down the hall and into Molly's bedroom. There, they rolled on the bed, laughing hysterically and telling each other to be quiet.

"She believed it," said Nell. "You could tell."

"Tigerel!" Molly shrieked. "What kind of name is Tigerel? There isn't any such name."

"I thought it sounded good," Nell replied. "Anyway, we have more to do now."

They went back up to the attic to search through the trunks. "There are some more costumes stored in the theater," Molly pointed out.

"I think we can find what we need here," said Nell.

And they did—enough clothes to make a sailor's outfit. Luckily, they also came across a jar of makeup that glowed in the dark. It had been used for the ghost scenes in *Hamlet*.

"Look at this!" Molly called as she came across a treasure packed in an old hatbox. Nell

came to look. It was a skull. "And wait
. . . you haven't seen the best part," said
Molly. She lifted off the top of it. There,
inside, were two candles behind the eye
sockets.

"Now all we need is some pieces of
red glass," said Nell. Triumphantly, Molly
picked them out of the bottom of the hatbox. They fit perfectly into the sockets. "Grandpa
must have had a wonderful time with this," Nell
said.

"Not as good as we will," Molly replied.

As it turned out, they really did spend most of
the afternoon sewing. Every now and then, Molly
would go down the hall and bat a tennis ball off
the wall. They didn't want Harriet to take a nice,
refreshing nap while it was still daytime.

At dinner, Harriet practically dozed off into
her dessert plate. But Nell and Molly begged her
to come into the parlor and use the Ouija board
once again. "Maybe there will be a message from
Tigerel," Molly said.

Nell gave her a nudge. "The others don't
know about Tigerel," she murmured.

"Well . . . a message from somebody."

No such luck. The spirits didn't seem to be
talkative tonight, at least when Harriet was using
the Ouija board. Once, when Molly and Nell had
their fingers on the planchette, it spelled out

"WHERE ARE MY . . . " But Harriet took the board away from them before the message could finish.

She tucked it under her arm and said she was going up to her room.

"I hope you'll sleep better tonight," Mother said.

"I feel like I could sleep for two nights," Harriet replied.

Nell and Molly excused themselves soon afterwards. They went to Molly's room to discuss strategy. The master bedroom where Harriet was sleeping had two glass doors that opened onto a balcony. "I'll wear the costume," said Molly. "I can climb onto the balcony from my bedroom window."

"We'll have to wait until everyone has gone to bed," said Nell.

"Agreed."

Fortunately, that wasn't very long. By the time the clock on Molly's wall read ten P.M., the house was silent and dark. They waited another fifteen minutes. Then Nell helped Molly put on the sailor suit and fit the skull atop her head. Nell carefully lit the candles and replaced the cap of the skull. She stepped back and shivered. The red-glass eyes glowed marvelously and with the additional head, Molly was nearly six feet tall. It was scary to look at, even when Nell knew it was only a stage trick.

"You look wonderful," she whispered. Her heart was beating the way it did backstage just before a play began.

They opened the window. Molly stepped outside. There was a wide ledge there, so she could easily walk across to the master bedroom balcony. Nell watched for a moment, and then got ready to do her part.

They had agreed to count to a hundred. By that time, Molly would certainly have time to reach the balcony. But of course, Harriet would be asleep. It was Nell's job to wake her up. She tiptoed down the hallway and turned the knob on Harriet's door.

The first thing she saw was Molly at the window—a tall sailor with glowing red eyes. Nell shivered. She went down on her hands and knees and crawled into the room. "Harriet," she cried in what she hoped was a ghostly voice, "Haa-aar-riet." No response. Maybe it hadn't been a good idea to keep her awake so long.

When Nell reached the foot of the bed, she began pulling the blanket.

"Mmf," said Harriet. Nell could feel the blanket tug back as Harriet tried to keep it. "Whatshap?"

Nell called again and heard Harriet sit up in bed. She must have opened her eyes at the same time, because there was a little gasp. Followed by one of the loudest shrieks Nell had ever heard—in or out of a theater. Almost at once, she heard something fly right over her and hit the floor running.

Harriet didn't notice that her bedroom door was already open. She was probably glad. Nell followed, and made it back to Molly's bedroom just in time to help her out of the costume and hide it in the closet.

The next morning, Bridget told them that Harriet had gone back to New York City. Bridget was annoyed. "She made Michael get out of bed in the middle of the night and drive her to the train station." Bridget said. "That girl thinks everyone should be at her beck and call. Hmp! And they say the rich have fine manners!"

A New Idea for a Play

APRIL 9, 1912

"RICHARD'S APPARENTLY DONE QUITE WELL IN England," said Nell's father. The family and their guest were seated around the dinner table. "I received a telegram from him today."

"Are they coming home soon?" asked Mama.

"They're leaving tomorrow on that new ship . . . the *Titanic.*"

"Oh!" said Freddy. "I'd love to be on it. That's the largest ship ever built. And they say the most luxurious one too. This will be its maiden voyage–the first trip it's ever made. Everybody who's rich has booked passage."

WESTERN UNION
TELEGRAM

TO: WILLIAM ALDRICH

ALDRICH HOUSE, LAKE RD.

LAKE CHOHOBEE VILLAGE,

MAINE, USA

LONDON, APRIL 9, 1912

LEAVING ENGLAND WITH LAURA APRIL 10

ON SHIP TITANIC STOP DUE IN NEW

YORK APRIL 14 STOP GREAT SUCCESS

AND MUCH TO TELL YOU STOP

RICHARD

Rocco shook his head. "Why would anyone rich want to go across the ocean?" he asked.

"Oh," Father said, "it's a wonderful trip—just like a floating resort if you're in first class. The finest food and wines, entertainment—" He stopped. Nell had seen Mother nudge his arm. "Of course, your trip may have been different—" Father began again, but this time gave a little grunt before he stopped. Nell knew Mother had kicked him under the table.

"It will be exciting to see if I can pick up radio messages from the *Titanic*," said Freddy. "Would you like to listen with me, Rocco?"

Rocco glanced nervously at Freddy. "I don't think so," he replied.

"When are you going to plant the tomatoes outside?" Nell asked Rocco. She wanted to change the subject.

Great-aunt Zena piped up from the other end of the table. "It can't be done until there's no danger of frost. Here in Maine, the temperature can go that low even in May."

"I open the window on sunny days," said Rocco. "To let the plants know what is coming."

"When do you expect we'll be able to eat tomatoes?" Mother asked him.

Rocco thought. "The plants are in the ground at the end of May," he said. He counted on his fingers. "Maybe end of July or beginning of August the fruit is ripe."

"By then, we'll be into the theater season too," said Father. "Has anyone started writing a play yet?"

"Well," Peggy replied, "it looked for a while as if we were going to write it on spiritualism. But now that Harriet has left—"

"It's really too bad she did," said Father.

Nell stared at him in surprise. "Oh, *no*, Father," she blurted out.

He nodded. "I know that she seemed a little . . . fascinated by the spirit world. But she seemed willing to back the summer performance. Her father is quite well off. The family made money in the railroad boom."

"Haven't we got enough money to do it ourselves?" asked Peggy.

Father smiled and pointed to the telegram. "If what Richard says is true, I guess we do. But it takes a great deal of money to maintain this house and open the theater for the summer. We couldn't do it if Richard and Laura didn't contribute so much."

"We could always charge admission this year," Molly pointed out.

"Your grandfather didn't want to do that," Father said. "He wanted to let the people of the town know what real theater was like."

"Most of them would rather go to the movies," said Polly.

"But that is the point, dear," replied Aunt Maud. "Lionel wanted people to see how much better the theater is than movies."

"I don't think movies are so bad," Nell remarked.

All the adults gave her disapproving looks. She blushed and didn't say anything more. But she had seen movies that were more exciting than a lot of plays. It was true, you couldn't hear what the actors in a movie were saying. On the other hand, you could see their faces much closer than on a stage. Movies were different, that's all, she thought. So there was no sense arguing with Mother, Father, and Aunt Maud. They were theater people.

Peggy spoke up. "Some well-known actors from the theater have started to appear in movies."

"Nobody first-rate," said Father firmly. "A movie producer actually made an offer to your Uncle Richard last year. Offered him a ton of money. Richard thought it was a great joke."

"Please," said Mother, "let's not talk about movies any longer. What are we going to present this summer?"

"I was thinking of writing a play that would make it clear that women should have the right to vote," said Peggy.

A silence fell over the table. Finally Mother asked, "Do you think that's the sort of thing our summer theater should be doing?"

"I believe in it," Peggy said, her chin high. "Don't you?"

"I guess I do," Mother said. "But—"

"You do?" interrupted Father.

"Why, yes," said Mother. "I think women are as capable of voting intelligently as men are."

Father reddened. "Well, when you put it like that—"

"What other way would you put it?" said Aunt Maud.

Father put up his hands. "No other way. But a political play . . . Do you really think Lionel would approve?"

Aunt Maud

"Of course he would." They all turned and looked at Great-aunt Zena, who usually fell asleep in her chair after dinner. "Lionel intended to educate people," she said, "not just entertain them."

"I'm not so sure of that," Father objected mildly. "Why don't we ask the children what they think? Nell? Do you want to be in a play about the right to vote?" The way he said it made it seem dull.

"I'm not sure," Nell said, with a quick look at Peggy. "I just wonder if you could make it interesting."

"A good writer can make any topic interesting," Peggy retorted.

"Not if it's going to be full of a lot of boring speeches," said Molly. "I want to see something *happen*."

"Excuse me," came a soft voice from the other end of the table. They were all surprised to hear Rocco speak up. "I know . . . " he began, "I am not a member of your family and it is not my place to speak."

"No, no," came a chorus of voices. "It's fine," said Mother. "We would love to hear your opinion, Rocco."

"You know," he said shyly, "I was in the strike at Lawrence." Mother and Father exchanged glances, and nodded. Nell guessed they must have known all along that Rocco was a striker.

Rocco spread his hands wide. "If a strike is to succeed, it must have all the people join in, you see? But the workers . . . not everybody is the same. Some Italian like me, some Jews, some Greeks, Syrians—come from everywhere."

"What does this have to do with our play?" asked Molly.

He waved a finger at her. "See, that is one way we brought people together. We put on plays at night. To show why we fighting. Plays were fun to watch. They had songs and music, so the audience joined in. It made them feel part of the One Big Union."

"Songs," Father said, with a snap of his fingers. "We haven't done a musical play in a long time."

"But how could you write songs for a political play?" objected Molly.

"Oh, that's the easiest thing in the world," Father replied. "Every presidential candidate has a campaign song, doesn't he? Songs and politics go together like—"

"Syrup and hot cakes," said Freddy.

"Sunshine and summer," said Molly, almost at the same time.

"There, you see?" said Father. "Everybody has some lyrics for a song. Now we've just got to put them together. Rocco, you've given us a great idea."

They got started that very night. In the parlor, Aunt Maud sat down at the piano and started to pick out tunes that the others hummed. Then somebody would try to match words to the music.

Peggy began to make a list of characters and who would play them. There was the heroic suffragette—herself, of course. Then the powerful politician who was opposed to women voting. That would be Uncle Nick's part. He would come back from New York City for the summer play. He loved to act with his children, Polly, Molly, and Freddy. Although in the play he would

Uncle Nick

be a nasty old man—maybe the suffragette's father? The suffragette might be a schoolteacher. Maybe she would have a boyfriend. . . .

"Are Harry and Jack going to be in the play?" she asked.

"Harry's planning to race cars all summer," said Father. "And Jack probably will stay in Germany to study."

"Aren't they even coming for the Fourth?" It was a tradition that the Aldriches gathered at Lake Chohobee every Fourth of July and New Year's Eve.

"Well, the family is larger now," said Father. "It's harder to bring everyone together at the same time. Neither of them has shown much interest in the theater lately."

Peggy tapped her pencil on the pad of paper. "It will be bad luck if they don't come," she said.

Night Messages

APRIL 12–13, 1912

FREDDY HAD FINALLY PERSUADED ROCCO TO COME upstairs and listen to the wireless radio. Because there was only one set of earphones, Freddy was using the loudspeaker so both of them could hear the signals.

It didn't make much difference to Rocco, since he couldn't understand the Morse code. It was all clicks and ticks to him. He yawned. It was way past his bedtime and they were the only people in the house who were still awake.

"The later it gets, the clearer the signals come in," Freddy told him. Freddy had no trouble understanding the code. The pad of paper in front of him was covered with messages that he had jotted down as they came in. Many of the people who sent them were regular friends of his. They liked to chat and exchange news. One friend sent the score of the New York Giants baseball game that day. In return, Freddy told him that the Boston Red Sox had beaten the New York Highlanders—something Freddy learned from Michael, who had gone to the game on his day off.

None of this was interesting to Rocco, but he was fascinated by how fast Freddy operated the telegraph key. Barely moving his hand up and down, he produced a steady stream of clicks. In his head, he translated incoming clicks into letters and words, writing them down as fast as he could.

"It would be easier if you could just say the message like on the telephone," said Rocco.

"That has already been done," Freddy replied. "But it takes a much more powerful transmitter than this one."

"Transmitter?"

Freddy tapped the box in front of him. "This thing. It sends the sound of the clicks through the air so other people can hear them."

Some more clicks came sputtering out of the loudspeaker. Freddy adjusted a knob to bring the signal in clearly. Then he sent a message of his own. "That sounds like the lighthouse keeper at Sable Island. He is in a great position to hear ships coming across the Atlantic. He's a friend of mine."

Rocco laughed. "Now I think you joke me," he said. "How can you tell one man's click from another?"

"Oh, you can," said Freddy. "It's the way they send. How fast, how slow. There's a certain style that you can recognize, like a person's voice." He held up his hand. "Listen!"

Rocco shook his head. All he could hear were clicks, but Freddy wrote something down. "He's giving me the frequency of the *Titanic*'s radio," he said. "Hooray! If we're lucky, we'll hear a message from the ship." He looked at the clock. "But it's already after midnight. Some of the ship operators go to bed when it's this late."

"Where is the ship now?" asked Rocco. "Close to land, yes?"

"No, oh, no . . . It's still out in the middle of the ocean."

The thought made Rocco a little dizzy. He remembered the middle of the ocean too well. When his mother became ill, it took a long time to find a doctor for her on the ship. Something in the drinking water had made many people sick. The doctor had given medicine to the passengers on the top deck—first-class passengers, Rocco was told. First-class passengers were treated first.

Down in the bottom of the ship—the steerage—Rocco and his mother slept in a big room with dozens of other people. Most of them were Italians, and they were kind to Mama. They gave her food, but she couldn't keep it down. An old woman cut up slivers of garlic and placed them in Mama's mouth. Nothing helped.

That was when Mama looked at Rocco and told him he was a good boy. And then she put her head back and closed her eyes.

The ship had no room for people who died at sea. The other passengers explained to Rocco what that meant. In the morning, some women wrapped Mama in a blanket and the men carried her up on deck. The ship had no priest, so someone said a few prayers. Rocco tried to pray too, but his brain had frozen. He looked at everything and understood it, but could not speak.

All he could think of was that if he'd been a really good boy, he would have found a way to keep Mama from dying.

A sailor sewed ballast stones into the blanket so that the body wouldn't float. Then they just put her over the side of the ship. Rocco put his hands over his ears now—just as he had then. But he could still hear the splash.

In the middle of the ocean. That was where his mother was. Not even in the cemetery next to the church with Rocco's three sisters. Just . . . some place Rocco would never be able to find again.

"That's strange," said Freddy. Rocco blinked his eyes, and stood up. "I go to sleep now," he said. He didn't want to hear any messages from people in the middle of the ocean.

"No, wait," Freddy called. "I'm getting . . . look at this." He pointed to the paper in front of him. He had written down three letters:

C Q D

Rocco shook his head. He had learned to read some things, but this was a word he'd never seen. He tried to pronounce it, but couldn't.

"No, it's not a word," Freddy explained. "That's ship code. It means . . . Come Quick, Disaster."

Rocco felt his body turn cold. "I do not want to hear any more," he said.

"No, I'm sure it's only a joke," Freddy said. "The lighthouse keeper must have given me the wrong frequency."

Freddy's hand sent out a chatter of Morse code. He waited a second, and then a message came back. "The lighthouse keeper thinks *I'm* the joker," he said. "He didn't receive the CQD message at all."

Freddy sat and listened for a while. Aside from the usual squeals and static, nothing came out of the loudspeaker. He turned the knob and tried different frequencies.

"Turn it off," Rocco said.

Freddy turned to look at him. "If it's really a distress call, I have to stay here. It's the duty of a wireless operator to pass on important messages."

Just then, a stream of code sounded again, very faintly. Freddy adjusted the controls. "That

Shipboard telegraph operator

sounds like the same operator—the one who's supposed to be on the *Titanic.*" He wrote down notes on his pad.

"Ice," he murmured. "Iceberg. He says the ship has hit an iceberg." Briefly, he signaled back, "Message received." Then he turned a dial and began sending again. A pause, then a return message.

"The lighthouse keeper heard it too," said Freddy. "This time he received the CQD message."

They waited for a few more minutes. The silence was broken by the clatter of code messages. Freddy kept writing them down. "The *Titanic* is trying to find out if there are any ships close by," he explained. "I should stay off the air so I won't confuse them."

Rocco sat down again. His stomach was tight. He wanted to go to bed and not listen any more. But he couldn't pull himself away. He thought about a whole ship of people in the middle of the ocean. The ocean that was so deep that if you sank, no one would ever find you again.

More code, and Freddy gasped when he heard it. "They've changed the message to SOS," he said. "And the operator says they're putting lifeboats in the water."

"Lifeboats?"

"Rocco," said Freddy, "maybe you should go downstairs and wake up Uncle William."

"What?" Rocco couldn't imagine doing such a thing.

"I can't believe it myself," Freddy said. "But the wireless operator believes the *Titanic* is sinking."

Rocco did not know how to respond. "Maybe it won't," he said. "Very big ship, yes? Should float long time."

"It's not supposed to be able to sink at all," Freddy replied. "But the wireless operator is only allowed to use the SOS message if the ship is in danger. That's a signal for every other ship to come immediately."

"Are they coming?" asked Rocco. "Can you hear?"

"The nearest ship is too far away," Freddy told him. "It won't be there for hours."

More code came from the speaker, and Freddy turned back to listen. "Another SOS," he said. "They're desperate. Please, Rocco. Go down and wake Uncle William. I've got to stay by the wireless."

Rocco took a deep breath. It was his duty, he told himself. He left the room and started downstairs.

TEN

Waiting for the News

APRIL 13–18, 1912

FOR A FEW DAYS, THERE WAS HOPE. THE FAMILY tried to find out every bit of news they could. In the beginning, Freddy supplied most of the information. The last wireless signal from the *Titanic* came at 2:10 A.M. It said that the crew had managed to get most of the lifeboats into the water.

"Richard and Laura might be in one of them," said Freddy's Aunt Anna. She had come upstairs with Uncle William and Freddy's mother, Maud, to listen to the messages.

Uncle William smiled grimly. "Not Richard," he said. "The rule of the sea is women and children first on the lifeboats. Richard wouldn't get into one as long as anybody else was on board."

"And Laura wouldn't go unless he did," added Aunt Anna.

A little after four A.M. Freddy took down a message from the *Carpathia,* a ship that had steamed to the rescue. "Its crew has picked up one of the lifeboats," said Freddy. "They're looking for others."

"It's good that some are safe," said Uncle William. "But there won't be any names of survivors for days. Perhaps we should all go to bed."

"I couldn't sleep anyway," Freddy said.

He did though. Later that morning, his mother brought a breakfast tray to the playroom. She found both Rocco and Freddy asleep in their chairs next to the wireless set. She covered them with blankets and tiptoed away.

The morning newspaper had nothing about the disaster. Uncle William tried to use the telephone to call the New York office of the White Star Line, the *Titanic*'s owners, but the line was always busy.

Around noon Freddy woke up and started hearing from other wireless operators. "They say the *Carpathia* is headed for New York," he reported. "It should be there in three days."

"I had better take the train to New York," said Uncle William. "I can be there before the ship arrives. I'll send a telegram after I find out."

For the next two days, the newspapers were filled with stories about the tragedy. One said that there were at least 700 survivors aboard the *Carpathia*.

"Seven hundred," said Nell at dinner. "That's a lot. I'm sure Uncle Richard and Aunt Laura must be safe."

"But there were over 2,200 people on the *Titanic*," Freddy told her. "That means more than twice 700 are missing."

Rocco shook his head, trying to wipe out the images that were inside. "No more! Please, no more!" he cried.

No one in the family really wanted to know anything more—except whether Richard and Laura were safe. People walked around the house aimlessly. No one played the piano after dinner. Great-aunt Zena took to her bed. Freddy stayed by the radio constantly. Aunt Maud and Aunt Anna tried to sew, but they found themselves staring out the window. When Polly tried to get someone to help her look for flies, they told her to stop bothering them. She went to her room to cry and Aunt Maud had to ask Molly to go comfort her.

Nell wandered outside one day and found Rocco working in the garden. "Is it time to plant the tomatoes yet?" she asked.

"No," he said. "Nights are too cold still."

"So what are you doing?"

"I am doing same as everybody else," he said. "I try to work at something so my brain is too busy to think."

"Why?" she asked. "You don't even know Uncle Richard and Aunt Laura."

"That is true," he said. "But I know what it is like to lose a person in the middle of the ocean."

She watched him dig. His life had been so very different from hers, she realized. She had grown up in this family that protected her, provided whatever she needed. Rocco was the same age as she was, had no one in the world, and he had already earned his own living. He had grown up, really.

"How did you . . . go on after your mother died?" Nell asked.

He looked at her. "That is what she wanted me to do," he said.

April 18 arrived, and Freddy's wireless friends told him the *Carpathia* had reached New York City. All that day, the Aldriches waited for the doorbell to ring. That would mean the Western Union telegram from Uncle William had arrived.

But it didn't. Now they had something new to worry about. Where was William? The next morning's newspaper carried a partial list of the survivors aboard the *Carpathia*. Eagerly, the Aldriches read through the long list of names, but no Aldrich was among them.

"There's still a chance," Nell said hopefully, but the house became even more gloomy.

The New York Times.

THE WEATHER.

Unsettled Tuesday; Wednesday, fair, cooler; moderate northerly winds, becoming variable.

VOL. LXI...NO. 19,886.

NEW YORK, TUESDAY, APRIL 16, 1912.—TWENTY-FOUR PAGES.

ONE CENT

TITANIC SINKS FOUR HOURS AFTER HITTING ICEBERG;
866 RESCUED BY CARPATHIA, PROBABLY 1250 PERISH;
ISMAY SAFE, MRS. ASTOR MAYBE, NOTED NAMES MISSING

Col. Astor and Bride, Isidor Straus and Wife, and Maj. Butt Aboard.

"RULE OF SEA" FOLLOWED

Women and Children Put Over in Lifeboats and Are Supposed to be Safe on Carpathia.

PICKED UP AFTER 8 HOURS

Vincent Astor Calls at White Star Office for News of His Father and Leaves Weeping.

FRANKLIN HOPEFUL ALL DAY

Manager of the Line Insisted Titanic Was Unsinkable Even After She Had Gone Down.

HEAD OF THE LINE ABOARD

J. Bruce Ismay Making First Trip to Olycelle Ship That Was to Surpass All Others.

Biggest Liner Plunges to the Bottom at 2:20 A. M.

RESCUERS THERE TOO LATE

Except to Pick Up the Few Hundreds Who Took to the Lifeboats.

WOMEN AND CHILDREN FIRST

Cunarder Carpathia Rushing to New York with the Survivors.

SEA SEARCH FOR OTHERS

The California Stands By on Chance of Picking Up Other Boats or Rafts.

OLYMPIC SENDS THE NEWS

Only Ship to Flash Wireless Messages to Shore After the Disaster.

The Lost Titanic Being Towed Out of Belfast Harbor.

CAPT. E. J. SMITH,
Commander of the Titanic.

PARTIAL LIST OF THE SAVED.

Includes Bruce Ism ,y, Mrs. Widener, Mrs. H. B. Harris, and an incomplete name, suggesting Mrs. Astor's.

CAPE RACE, N. F., Tuesday, April 16.—Following is a partial list of survivors among the first-class passengers of the Titanic, received by the Marconi wireless station this morning from the Carpathia, via the steamship Olympic:

Just after lunch, the front door did open. The family had gathered in the solarium to catch the spring sunshine. But a chill went through everyone as William appeared in the doorway.

His face showed them all they needed to know. It was gray and drawn. He looked as if he'd grown years older in the few days since they'd seen him last. His hair, usually so neat and brushed, hung over his forehead.

He slumped into a chair and looked at them. "You might as well all know," he said. "They're lost. Everything is lost."

No one spoke for a second. Then Aunt Maud asked, "Are you sure? The newspapers said there may be more survivors on other ships."

He nodded. "I spoke to a woman who was in one of the lifeboats. It was just as we thought. Richard remained aboard the *Titanic* because there weren't enough lifeboats for all the passengers. And Laura wouldn't leave him. She gave her seat in a lifeboat to this woman. The woman had a young child, and Laura said to her, 'My sons are grown, they'll get along.'"

Everyone sat stunned by the news. Finally William spoke again: "That isn't all."

It wasn't? Nell wondered. What more could there be? They all looked at each other. "I saw Richard's business agent," her father said, "because I thought we should arrange a memorial service."

"Yes, that's what we must do," said Aunt Maud.

"But he told me . . . " William paused and unloosened the knot of his tie. Everyone was surprised. He *never* did that while he was downstairs. Clearing his throat, he went on. "The agent said that Richard was carrying all the money he and Laura had made on their European trip."

Another silence fell. The children didn't quite understand. "Why would he bring all that money with him?" Nell asked. "He could have put it in a bank."

"Richard didn't trust banks," her father answered. "Not since the Panic of 1907, when he lost money in a bank that failed. He had telegraphed the agent that he was going to leave the money with him after they arrived in New York."

"So that means . . . " Aunt Maud began.

"I don't know what we're going to do," said Father. "We can't keep up the house without the money Richard contributed."

"What about the summer theater?" Peggy asked.

"There's enough to get us through the end of the year," said her father. "But if we cancel the summer theater . . . we can afford the house a bit longer. By that time, maybe . . . "

"No," said Nell. She was thinking about what Rocco had said the other day. "Papa," she said, "you know what Uncle Richard would want."

Her mother nodded. "It's true, William," she said. The others chimed in with their opinions: "That's right . . . we must . . . the show must go on."

Their reaction seemed to make Nell's father feel better. "Of course," he said. "Even if it's the last season for the theater, we'll dedicate it to Richard and Laura."

A Memorial to Remember

AT THE HOUSE

AFTERWARD

IT WAS A LOVELY DAY FOR THE SERVICE, EVERYBODY agreed. The sun was shining in a bright blue sky that reflected off the lake. The air was almost as warm as summer, and the trees had put forth their bright green leaves. It was what people called a Real Maine Day. Tears came to Nell's eyes as she caught herself enjoying the weather. Uncle Richard and Aunt Laura would have loved it too.

Nell walked through the crowd that had gathered at the edge of the lake. She recognized many of the people who were there. Almost anybody would have known them. They were famous

Memorial Service for

Richard and Laura Aldrich

AT ALDRICH HOUSE
JUNE 1, 1912
11 A.M.

RECEPTION

actors and actresses, people who had appeared in plays all over the United States. The Barrymores, the Powers, John Drew, Lillian Russell, George M. Cohan, Sarah Bernhardt, George Arliss—some of the most handsome and beautiful people in the whole country.

Best of all, everybody in the family showed up. Uncle Nick, the father of Freddy and the twins, let his understudy take over his part in New York. And Nell's cousins Harry and Jack finally arrived in Harry's new red Bugatti. Of course they were Richard and Laura's sons, so everybody expected they would be there.

"If they're the same as ever," Peggy said, "Jack will blow something up and Harry will crash his car into a tree."

They had something even more spectacular planned. After a friend of Laura's sang "We Shall Gather at the River," Jack read a few of his father's favorite speeches from Shakespeare. He finished with the lines from *Hamlet*: "Goodnight, sweet prince / May flights of angels sing thee to thy rest." No one had ever thought Jack much of an actor, but he read so well that people in the crowd were silently crying.

Then Harry stepped forward and

Jack

127

looked toward the far end of the lake. In the silence, a buzzing noise could be heard in the distance. It sounded like a swarm of bumblebees, but grew louder and louder.

A murmur ran through the crowd as an airplane came into view. It was a biplane, with an open cockpit between the two wings. As the plane flew past the beach, Nell recognized the pilot.

"It's Uncle Georgie," she whispered to Peggy. Peggy just shook her head. Georgie was the oddball of the family—always experimenting with whatever was new, always failing in some spectacular fashion.

Nell knew that Georgie had been taking flying lessons, but she had no idea he intended to use them at the memorial. Jack and Harry, however, had evidently been in on the plan. Harry began to read in

Harry

a voice loud enough to be heard over the plane's engine. He quoted from a long poem Nell had heard Father read parts of in the evenings. Harry finished with the lines, "Each Morn a thousand Roses brings, you say; / Yes, but where leaves the Rose of Yesterday? / And this first Summer month that brings the Rose / Shall take Father and Mother away."

As he stopped, Harry signaled to the pilot and a stream of rose petals flew out of the cockpit. They scattered onto the lake, making beautiful red drops on the dark blue water.

It was so spectacular a scene that many of those in the crowd broke into applause. "It takes a lot to impress these people," Peggy whispered.

That would have been a brilliant finish to the ceremony, but Uncle Georgie couldn't live with success. Trying for an even more impressive display, he turned the plane around and headed down the beach again. As he passed by, he sent the plane sharply upward. Just as it seemed he could go no higher, he tipped it over backwards so that he was flying upside down. People gasped, but Nell saw that he intended to do a loop in the air.

Uncle Georgie

Unfortunately, he'd forgotten to fasten his seat belt—at least, that's how Harry explained it afterward. So when the plane flipped over, Uncle Georgie fell out of the cockpit. The plane roared past the spectators with him hanging on desperately to the steering gear.

Not for long. His hands slipped and he fell from the sky, hitting the lake with a loud splash. People were screaming now. Some were pointing to the spot where Uncle Georgie had disappeared. Others to the plane, which was headed up the lake upside down and pilotless.

Jack and Harry took control of the situation. They launched a small boat from the dock. By this time, luckily, Georgie had come to the surface and was calling for help. They rowed out and soon lifted him into the boat.

Meanwhile, the plane, finding itself without a pilot, lazily swept downward and landed on the surface of the lake like a clumsy seagull. As the wings hit the water, they crumpled a bit and the plane twisted to a stop.

The unusual end to the memorial service gave everybody something to talk about at the reception. The gloomy mood that had hung over the house for weeks seemed to dissipate like a fog. Georgie was brought into the house, soaked but looking no more dazed than usual. Everybody rushed to congratulate him on his daring feat.

While the attention was on Georgie, Harry walked into the ballroom. Nell thought he looked more handsome than ever. She went over to him, wondering if he would stay for the rest of the summer. Lionel Barrymore reached Harry first. "That was something Richard would have enjoyed seeing," said the famous actor. He clapped Harry on the shoulder. "Fine job of reading, son," he said. "Your father couldn't have done better."

Harry reddened at the praise. Peggy had once told Nell that Harry hated the fact that people always compared him to his father.

Nell changed the subject. "Are you going to stay and be in our summer theater production?" she asked him.

"Oh, I don't think so," Harry said. "I've got some auto races to enter. I'm missing the big one in Indianapolis this weekend."

"You were very good in the play two summers ago," Nell told him. "The one where you played an Arab prince."

He smiled at her. "I enjoy racing cars more. There's nothing like the feeling of speed. I'll give you a ride around the lake in the Bugatti, if you'd like."

Nell shivered. "Peggy says she once beat you around the lake on a horse."

Harry nodded ruefully. "That's true. But she

wouldn't do it today. Cars have improved, but horses haven't. That Bugatti can go over 100 miles an hour. No horse could come close to it."

Lionel Barrymore was listening intently. "When I was your age," he told Harry, "I didn't think I'd be an actor, either. My parents were too famous. I studied to be a painter, and then a composer. But it's in your blood, young man. The stage pulls you back."

Lionel Barrymore

Harry looked away. "Maybe so," he said. He excused himself and went off to greet other guests.

Nell had something she wanted to ask Mr. Barrymore. "What do you think of the movies?"

"What do I think of 'em?" he replied. "Why, they're shoddy, cheap, and vulgar. Not to mention you can't hear a thing the actors are saying."

Nell was disappointed. "I see," she said. "I guess you think no first-rate actor would be in a movie."

"Certainly not," he said, and then added with a twinkle in his eye, "Of course, I've been in a few."

"You have?"

"Yes, but they haven't put my name on the screen, so I'm not disgraced. I met this fellow Griffith. He's a director for Biograph, one of the big movie companies. He talked me into it. I suppose people will find out soon enough, because I'm in a major one coming out this year. It's called *The Musketeers of Pig Alley.*"

"But I thought you said no first-rate actor—"

"Oh, pish-tosh," he replied. "Actors have always acted wherever people wanted to see them. You have to make some money or you'd starve." He snorted. "I found that out when I tried to be a painter."

He gave Nell a look. "I haven't seen you act yet," he said. "You thinking of going into the movies?"

She blushed. "I don't know if I could," she said.

"Oh, you're an Aldrich. Of course you could," he said. "I tell you what. When does this summer theater start?"

"It opens July Fourth," she told him.

He winked at her. "Maybe—just maybe—I can persuade Griffith to come up and take a look. He was a theater person originally. He knows talent."

"That would be wonderful," she said. "I don't know how to thank you."

"Be as good an actress as you can be," he said.

TWELVE

A Lot of Endings

ROCCO PROMISED NELL THAT SHE COULD TASTE the first ripe tomato. Never before had Nell watched anything grow so closely. In summers past, she had picked flowers from the gardens to make little bouquets. But she didn't visit them day by day. With the tomatoes, she did.

In early June she saw the plants sprout small yellow blossoms. Rocco pointed out the bees that spread pollen from flower to flower. And as soon as the petals wilted, tiny green tomatoes appeared in their place.

It seemed to take forever for them to grow to full size and then ripen. Nell was so eager to pick one that she found a recipe in the library for fried green tomatoes.

Rocco shook his head. "Not the first ones," he said. "Maybe the ones at the end of the summer because there are too many then anyway. But the first ones . . . you must eat ripe."

As soon as the tomatoes were the least bit pink, she wanted to eat them. But Rocco said no. Until yesterday, when he said the tomatoes would be ready to pick. Tomorrow.

"Tomorrow?" she said. "July Fourth? That's the day the play opens."

"It's okay," he told her. "Tomatoes should be picked early in the morning anyway. That's when they have the most flavor."

"How early?" she asked.

"Very early."

So just as the sun turned the sky from black to pink, Nell and Rocco went around to the back of the house. She hadn't bothered to put on shoes because she intended to go right back to bed. The dew on the grass was cool and tickled her feet.

It was strange being up so early. Not even the birds were awake yet. Through the pine trees down by the lake, she could see that mist still covered the water. It was like being in a fairy tale, where she and Rocco were lost in the forest.

Rocco stepped aside to let her see the tomato plants. In the morning light, everything else seemed grayish green. But the bright red fruits blazed as if they were magic.

He pointed to one of them. "Pick that one," he said. "Just hold it on the bottom and twist," turning his own wrist to show her how.

She cupped the tomato in her hand. It felt warmer than the air. It dropped off the plant as if it had been waiting for her.

Rocco had brought a knife. He took hold of Nell's hand, and as she unfolded her fingers, he sliced the tomato in half. Surprised, she felt the blade just touch her palm without hurting her.

He took half the tomato and held it under his nose. "Smell," he said.

She did the same with her half. An aroma that was sweet and fresh and tart arose from the moist tomato.

Closing his eyes, Rocco bit into the tomato. Giggling, Nell did too, feeling as if they had stolen the fruit and were trying to eat it before anybody found them.

Juice flowed down her chin, and she leaned forward so that it wouldn't run onto her robe. The tomato really did taste—as Rocco had promised—like nothing she had ever eaten. It reminded her of things that came from faraway places, too rich and full of spices to have grown here.

"That's the best thing I've ever tasted," she said.

He smiled, because he had wanted to give her something in return for what she had given him. And he smiled because the tomato reminded him of home, of Italy, of days lost in the past. That made him sad, and his eyes changed.

She saw the expressions on his face without knowing what they meant. He was a mystery to her, one she knew she would never solve.

"We should pick some more for your family," he said.

She nodded, thinking for a moment that she didn't want anyone else to have any.

He had brought a basket and, as they filled it, Nell said suddenly, "I just realized. I always wondered what it would be like to have a brother. I guess I know now."

"Freddy is like your brother," he said.

"Is he?" she replied in a disappointed voice. "Well, then I'd rather have a brother like you. And now I do."

Everybody else agreed that the tomatoes were delicious. But there was hardly time to enjoy them. The opening performance of the play was at one P.M. As soon as they finished breakfast, the Aldriches headed for the theater that Grandpa had built by the lake.

Peggy had written some crowd scenes into the play, and this year some of the townspeople would appear as extras. "There are going to be some surprised people in the audience," Peggy told Nell.

Nell herself was going to have the biggest role she'd ever played. She was going to be a little girl who starts people thinking by asking questions. The opening scene took place on election day. It was a big production, with people singing campaign songs and waving banners. A brass band would march across the stage as the candidates for mayor gave speeches.

But Nell brought the action to a standstill by asking, "Why do only men get to vote?"

She was a little nervous backstage, because she remembered Lionel Barrymore's promise. "Just maybe" the movie director Mr. Griffith would be in the audience.

"What's the matter?" asked Rocco. He was helping to move scenery.

"Can you tell I'm nervous?" she asked. "I'm not supposed to look nervous."

"You were in plays before, yes?"

"Yes, but I didn't have such a big part."

He shrugged. "It's only make . . ." He tried to think of the right word.

"Makeup?" she asked, puzzled.

"No, no, you know, it is when you pretend."

"Oh." She understood now. "Make-believe."

"Yes, that's right. Only make-believe, so it doesn't matter."

She laughed. "Well, if you look at it that way . . . I guess nobody in our family has done anything real for years."

He nodded. "All this—" He waved his arms, taking in the theater, the lake, the grounds, the house. "It doesn't seem real to me."

Nell felt better. She peeked through the curtains. The theater was full. Word had spread far beyond the town about the Aldrich Summer Theater. This year, they would stage three performances a week for the rest of the summer.

The music started, and everybody ran for their places. In a few minutes, Nell was standing in front of the footlights. She stared out, hoping to spot someone in the audience who looked like a movie director.

When she delivered her big line, there was a strange reaction. Some people applauded warmly. Then a few boos were heard. Nell was shocked. But she recovered at once. Without thinking, she stepped closer to the edge of the stage and repeated the line: "Why do only men get to vote?"

That brought on a volley of cheers that drowned out the boos. People stood up in their seats to applaud. Nell felt a glow as she realized what she'd done. She stood there, letting the applause wash over her.

From the wings, someone called her name. Nell

looked over. It was Peggy, waving her arms. "Get back!" she called. "We can't lower the curtain."

Nell realized she was in front of the curtain line. With a smile and a bow, she moved out of the way.

That was just the first act. As the second began, Nell's question started women in the imaginary town thinking. And then talking. Asking questions of their own. As the act went on, the women heard all the reasons why women shouldn't vote. It was no coincidence that those were the very same reasons listed on the handbill Marshall Pomeroy had given Peggy in his store.

In the play, the women didn't think those were such good reasons. By the end of the second act, they'd decided what to do. In a big song-and-dance number (called "No More Work") they told off the men of the town. The women announced they weren't going to work for the men any longer. They weren't going to cook, or clean, or mend their clothes, or keep house.

The big surprise for the audience *this* time was that many of the younger women of Lake Chohobee (the real town) appeared on stage. A shout of surprise, and then laughter, greeted each one as the audience recognized her. And the last one got the biggest shout. She was Angela Pomeroy, Marshall's sister and the daughter of

Lake Chohobee's mayor.

There was a lot of joking and giggling backstage between the second and third acts. The women in the play enjoyed the reaction of their friends and relatives out front. They kept peeking out into the audience to report what was going on. Arguments broke out. A few people stalked out of the theater. Others booed them as they left. There was so much commotion that the next act had to be delayed while the band played a tune to calm everybody down.

Finally the curtain rose, revealing a bleak scene. The make-believe mayor of the town in the play was trying to cook. The house was a mess. Dirty clothes were everywhere, and unwashed dishes were piled in the sink. Somebody was sitting in an easy chair near the front of the stage. The audience couldn't see who, because the person was holding a newspaper. But a stream of cigar smoke came drifting up from behind the paper, so everybody thought it was a friend of the mayor's.

Then the mayor, wearing an apron, came out to plead with the person for help. The newspaper slowly lowered, revealing who was behind it. It was Peggy, playing the part of the mayor's wife. She tapped her cigar ashes on the floor.

In the play, the men of the town eventually gave in, of course. There was a big finale with a parade of victorious women singing a rousing song. They were going to vote for the first time. The mayor's wife was running against him.

But the play ended before the votes were counted. Nell got to step forward for the very last line: "What kind of leaders would we have—if women could vote?"

The audience seemed surprised when the curtain came down. They weren't sure that was really the end of the play. They were still talking about it as they filed out of the theater and went up the hill to the lawn party.

Nell and Peggy stood next to the table with the punch bowl. Dozens of people came up to congratulate them and ask about the play's ending. "I wanted people to imagine for themselves what the ending should be," Peggy told them. Some were satisfied with this answer; others weren't.

One woman asked, "You mean whether the mayor or the mayor's wife won the election?"

"Not exactly," Peggy replied. "I meant to answer the questions that Nell asked, for themselves."

"I see," said the woman. "You know, I never thought women should get the vote. Didn't bother me. Because why are men going to give it to them? But your play . . . it makes you think, all right."

Peggy smiled.

A tall man wearing a floppy straw hat and a

gray linen suit walked up to them. Nell couldn't recall seeing him before. Some of the men in the audience were angry about the play. Marshall Pomeroy and his sister had been shouting at each other. Nell hoped this wasn't somebody else coming to complain.

But her knees got a little weak when he introduced himself. "I'm David Griffith," he said in a deep Southern accent. "Lionel Barrymore said I would enjoy myself if I came up to see your theater work. He didn't deceive me."

"Thank you," said Peggy. She didn't seem as excited as Nell. Maybe she didn't know who Mr. Griffith was.

He gave Nell a look down his long, sharp nose. "You displayed a good deal of poise and presence, young lady," he told her.

That sounded good, even if she wasn't exactly sure what he meant. "It's just make-believe," she said.

A smile came over his craggy face. Nell thought it looked like he didn't smile often. "I wonder if you've ever considered appearing in a motion picture play," he asked.

D.W. Griffith

Nell had to warn herself not to jump up and

down. "I'd love to try that," she replied in what she hoped was a calm voice. "But I have to get my parents' permission."

"Oh, I'll explain it to them," Peggy cut in.

"By the way," said Mr. Griffith as he turned toward Peggy, "The program doesn't say who the author of this play is."

"Oh, we all had a hand in it, as usual," Peggy said.

"Peggy's just being modest," said Nell. "She wrote just about all of it except the songs."

"We're always looking for writers," said Mr. Griffith. "Biograph makes ten or twelve new film plays a week."

"A week?"

"Yes, and the pay isn't what you'd get for a full-length play, but—"

"I'll come with Nell and give it a try," Peggy said. "What about adapting the play you just saw?"

Peggy and Mr. Griffith started to discuss screenwriting, and Nell slipped away. She felt like running and telling someone—Papa, Mama, or Rocco.

She ran around the corner of the house. And there, standing by the tomato plants, were all three of them. Along with another man, taller than Papa, and dressed in work clothes. Nell hardly noticed him. She was too excited.

"Mama! Papa!" she cried. "I have to tell you! Mr. Griffith is here and he's a friend of Lionel Barrymore's and he wants me to be in the movies!" She realized as she said it that Peggy would have found a better way to break the news.

"Nell," Mama said, "Where are your manners?" She gestured toward the strange man. "This is Mr. Vivanti, Rocco's father."

Rocco's father? Nell looked at the man, and then at Rocco. Yes, she could see the resemblance. But Rocco looked much more handsome . . . nicer. The man looked very worn-out, as if he'd worked too hard and too long.

"I'm pleased to meet you," she said politely.

Rocco's father nodded slightly and then turned to Nell's father. "I thank you so much again. I worried about Rocco. My friend not find him on the right day. But now . . . "

Rocco's Father

He put his hand on Rocco's shoulder. "We together." He gave Rocco a little push and said something to him in Italian. Rocco nodded and went off toward the house.

"You don't have to leave so soon," said Mother. "At least stay for dinner."

Rocco's father shook his head. "I have day off from work only today," he said.

Nell was trying to understand. Why did Rocco run inside if his father was leaving so soon?

"We'll have Michael drive you and Rocco to the train station as soon as Rocco has gathered his clothes," Father said.

"What?" cried Nell. "Rocco's leaving? Right now?"

"I know it's sudden," said Father. "But when you gave me the letter Rocco had, I wrote to the return address on it. After Mr. Vivanti learned that Rocco was safe with us, he decided to come get him."

Nell turned to Mr. Vivanti. "Can't Rocco stay for a while longer? Just the rest of the summer?"

Mr. Vivanti shook his head firmly. "Rocco should not be in a house like this. He stay too long already. Man I work for says he will give Rocco a job."

Nell stared at him. Then she turned and ran. She tried to think of a plan. Maybe she could let the air out of the tires on the car. Or suppose Rocco came down with a fever. They could put a hot water bottle on his forehead to make his temperature go up. . . .

By the time she reached the front door, Rocco was already coming out. He carried the same leather bag he had brought with him almost four months ago. Had it been only that long?

"Rocco," she said. "Come with me. I'll find a place for you to hide. Then, after your father has gone . . . ”

He took her hand. "No," he said. She could see that he was trying not to cry. He was being brave. That made her start to cry.

"What about . . . what about the tomatoes?" she said, sniffling.

"You will take care of them for me," he said. "And you must promise—"

"What?"

"Take the best ones and keep the seeds. Put them in a plate outside to dry on a sunny day. And then send them to me."

"How will I know where you are? You have to write me a letter."

"Yes, I will learn how to do that."

"I don't want you to go."

"It's what I told you," he said. "All this was just make-believe for me. I knew it would end."

"Oh!" she said. "I almost forgot." She began to cry harder. "I am going to be in the movies. Maybe."

He laughed. "Why would you cry at that? Then I will get to see you always."

"It's not the same. Promise me you'll come back."

He shook his head. "I can't."

"I'll find a way then," she said. "At least promise you won't forget me."

"Oh, I promise that," he said. "I will always remember."

"I will too," she told him. "And someday we'll be together again. We have to be."

He looked at her. "Why you so sure?"

"Because we were born together," she said.

A Few Historical Notes

The strike of textile workers in Lawrence, Massachusetts, in 1912 was led by members of the International Workers of the World (the IWW). The IWW wanted to organize all workers into "one big union" to give them more power. The strikers were primarily Italians, Jews, Syrians, and Poles. They succeeded because they cooperated in working together. Unlike other union organizations, the IWW welcomed members of any ethnic group. The idea worked at Lawrence, and the mill owners eventually gave the workers a raise in pay and better working conditions.

It is true that during the strike the police stopped workers from sending their children out of the city. The reason was that the first group of children to leave created sympathy for the strike elsewhere.

Congress passed a child-labor law in 1916, but the Supreme Court declared the law unconstitutional. A federal law preventing children under sixteen from working in factories did not come into effect until 1938. Even today, no law protects children from working at farm labor.

We wanted to find out the reasons why some people didn't want to allow women to vote. So we went to the New York Public Library and found a one-page flyer just like the one Marshall Pomeroy gave Nell and Peggy. In 1919, Peggy and the other suffragettes won their fight. In that year Congress finally passed a constitutional amendment giving women the right to vote. The amendment was ratified by the states the following year.

Ouija boards were popular in the nineteen-teens (1910–1919), and have come in and out of favor ever since. The name *ouija* comes from the French word *oui* and the German word *ja*. Both mean "yes." Messages from Ouija boards, as Rocco realized, are not sent by spirits.

The Youth's Companion, a children's magazine of the time, reported that the wireless distress signals from the *Titanic* were picked up by young amateur radio operators on the East Coast of the United States.

The New York Highlanders baseball team in the American League changed their name in 1913, when they became known as the Yankees.

All the actors mentioned in the story are real (except for the Aldriches). You can see Lionel Barrymore, his brother John, and his sister Ethel in many old movies. Drew Barrymore, one of today's screen stars, is the granddaughter of John Barrymore, and the grand-niece of Lionel. She is also related to the Drews, another famous American family of actors.

At the beginning of Chapter Seven, Molly says, "That should put her in a swivet." This was a slang expression of the time, meaning, "That should upset or confuse her." Someone asked us for the origin of the word *swivet*, but we couldn't find it in any dictionary. Maybe you'd like to do some detective work on it. If you find the origin, send us an e-mail at TandDHoob@aol.com.

Rocco Vivanti (1900–)

Lionel (1819–1902)

m

Richard (1866–1912)

Laura (1867–1912)

m

William (1867–)

m

Anna (1868–)

Harry (1887–)

Jack (1888–)

Peggy (1889–)

Nell (1900–)

Family

Adele (1838–1910)

Zena (1840–)

Maud (1872–)

m

Nick Woods (1870–)

George (1874–)

Molly (1898–)

Polly (1898–)

Freddy (1899–)

Things That Really Happened

1910

Airplanes have caught the public imagination. One of the top songs of the year is "Come, Josephine, in My Flying Machine."

The Boy Scouts of America are founded.

1911

Frances Hodgson Burnett publishes *The Secret Garden.*

On March 25, in New York City, a fire in the Triangle Shirtwaist Factory kills 146 women workers.

On May 30, the first Indianapolis 500-mile auto race is held.

1912

Oreo cookies are first sold.

New Mexico becomes the 47th state.

Arizona becomes the 48th state.

Woodrow Wilson is elected president.

The Girl Guides of America is founded; the following year the name is changed to the Girl Scouts.

The Olympics in Stockholm, Sweden, include women's events in swimming and diving for the first time. However, the head of the U.S. Olympic team refuses to allow American women to take part.

1913

LifeSavers candy (peppermint flavor) is first sold.

The 793-foot-high (242-meter) Woolworth Building opens in New York City. It will be the world's tallest building until 1930.

During the Years 1910–1919

California passes a law making it illegal for Japanese immigrants to own land.

Notre Dame becomes the first college football team to make extensive use of the forward pass as it defeats the Army team 35 to 13.

1914

On January 5, Henry Ford announces a minimum pay for his workers of $5 a day, for an eight-hour work shift. (This is a raise from $2.40 a day for a nine-hour shift.) The change makes it possible for the Ford factories to operate around the clock in three daily shifts.

New Jersey sets a minimum wage for women of $9 a week.

The Panama Canal is opened.

The first transcontinental telephone line is completed.

Gasoline companies begin to distribute road maps to customers.

The red-green traffic light is introduced in Cleveland, Ohio.

Congress passes a bill making the second Sunday in May Mother's Day.

World War I begins in Europe.

Charlie Chaplin first appears in a movie as the character "the little tramp." The character will make him one of the most popular movie stars of the century.

J. M. Ward invents the electric hand dryer for public bathrooms.

1915

On May 7, a German submarine sinks the British ship *Lusitania*. Among the passengers who die are 128 Americans. The United States government condemns Germany for its "unrestricted submarine warfare."

The first automobile taxicabs appear in American cities.

1916

On March 9, Mexican revolutionary Pancho Villa leads his soldiers in an attack on Columbus, New Mexico. Seventeen residents of the town are killed. President Wilson assigns General John J. Pershing to lead 15,000 troops into Mexico to capture Villa. The U.S. force returns empty-handed two years later.

Movie star Mary Pickford, known as "America's Sweetheart," signs a contract that will pay her over $1 million for the next two years. At the same time, Charlie Chaplin signs a similar contract for $10,000 a week.

President Wilson wins reelection after campaigning on the slogan, "He kept us out of war."

Jeannette Rankin of Montana becomes the first woman ever elected to Congress.

1917

On April 6, at the urging of President Wilson, Congress declares war on Germany.

The first recording of jazz music is made.

Clarence Birdseye develops a method of preserving foods by freezing them.

1918

On November 11, Germany agrees to cease fighting, bringing World War I to an end. For many years, the date is celebrated as Armistice Day. (Now it is called Veterans Day.)

For the first time, the United States sells special stamps for airmail delivery.

Spanish flu epidemic breaks out in the United States and continues through 1919. About 25 million people (one in every four) catch the disease, and 500,000 die from it. It is the worst epidemic in the country's history.

1919

The ice-cream bar on a stick is invented ("I-Scream-Bar").

On January 29, the 18th Amendment to the Constitution is ratified. This amendment prohibits the manufacturing, sale, and transportation of alcoholic beverages. It is the first amendment to restrict people's rights, rather than expand them.

On June 28, the leaders of the victorious nations in the world war sign the Versailles Treaty. It imposes harsh terms on Germany and calls for the establishment of a League of Nations.

The Cincinnati Reds defeat the Chicago White Sox in the World Series, five games to three. Later, it is discovered that several members of the White Sox were bribed by gamblers to throw the games. They become known as the Black Sox.

On November 19, the United States Senate refuses to ratify the Versailles Treaty.